Book ‹

1

The ancient bog

The shouting and screaming cut through the dark night like a knife.

The dark figure slipped through the trees and bushes looking over his shoulder. He was so pale you could see him in the moon light, and it was hard for him to hide. The villagers were getting closer, and the angry mob was after his blood. Well, he had taken so much of theirs already.

Then the pale figure carried on, and then stopped its feet were suck in the mud. It looked around wildly as it began to sink ever so slowly at first. Then the villagers came into the clearing, and saw the being in the mud. They cheered and watched as the figure sank.

They waved their wooden torches about, and slapped each other on the backs.

"The vampire is dead," they cheered as one.

The figure slowly sank until its head was the only thing left. It looked at the angry crowd with hate filled eyes, and cursed them in a foreign language.

Then it was gone, and the crowd began to walk back to the village.

Now

The small tree started to grow in the bog, and over a few years the tree got bigger.

It began to cover the surface of the bog until its branches were everywhere.

Adam was ten and Butler was nine, and they were playing ball by the bog. Adam had an Arsenal football club shirt on and black shorts he was a small boy with brown hair. He had a cute face, and looked like an angel people would say which he found rather irritating.

Butler was taller and fatter than his older friend. He had blonde hair, and beady little blue eyes he wore a track suit and trainers. Butler kicked the ball hard, and it went over Adams head, and into the trees and bushes.

"Damn sorry Adam," he called out.

"What do you want me to get that then," Adam said shrugging his shoulders.

"What scared of the trees," Butler laughed.

That was it then Adam had to go into the dark trees and bushes for the ball, or he would never live it down. Adam went into the gloomy darkness of the trees, and stepped over small bushes where was the ball. He saw the ball by another bush, and quickly went over and bent down. A small branch curled round his arm, and he cried out.

Then branches wrapped round his legs, and he felt pin pricks in his skin. He fell on his back and was dragged into the bog. Butler stood at the edge of the trees he had heard his friend cry out.

"Adam you okay in there," he called out.

He waited five minutes then ran home.

The police came later that day and searched the bog.

They were careful not to step into the bog, even though it looked all dried up now. No body was found, and they gave up after a few hours.

The boy Adams father came to the bog one afternoon he had been drinking with his mates. He was drunk as he was most days now, he missed his son. It had been two months since he had gone missing his wife was still on drugs to take the pain away. Life was one drinking binge after another now for

William. He was a thin man with grey hair that was rapidly receding.

He had wrinkles in his face, and looked a lot older than his fifty years. He had given up work he just could not face it anymore.

He stumbled into the bog and looked round, "Adam," he called out.

He was rocking and rolling and almost fell over, he leaned on a tree and sighed.

"Adam come home son," he whined.

Then something wrapped around his ankles, and he looked down in horror. Branches were wrapping round his legs, and then his arms were seized. He felt hundreds of pin pricks in his skin and cried out in pain. Soon he was wrapped up like a cocoon.

He was dragged along the ground, and into the bogs centre.

The plant that covered the bog began to flower that summer. It was an awesome sight it flowered in many colours, but its main colour was blood red. There were a herd of cattle in the field one day, and one strayed over to the bog area.

The red of the flowers seemed to glow in the sun light they were like small roses. The cow began to feed on the grass when its body was engulfed in branches. It was wrapped up like a present, and slowly pulled into the bog.

Farmer Tim was a no-nonsense kind of man, he was tall and thin, and wore a hat. He wore his work blue boiler suit, and sighed as he saw the cow being dragged into the bog.

"That bog is the work of the devil I have always said that," he said to himself.

Tim was sitting inside his tractor. He drove the tractor back to the farm, and loaded up a big barrel of petrol. He drove into the bog, and ploughed through the trees and bushes. He tipped the petrol as he went, and then came out the other side.

He jumped down from the tractors cab, and saw a flower on the side of his tractor.

It was moving even through its stem was broken off. It moved and he saw tiny white pin heads inside the flower and on the stem. It was an evil wicked looking thing close, and Tim shivered.

He walked to the edge of the bog, and threw his lighter into the trees, and stepped back. He watched as the bog went up in flames.

He got a stick and removed the flower from his tractor, and got in the cab and drove away. The bog would burn for hours because of the bog fuel as well.

The end

C Robert Paul Bennett 2016

2

The count

The car speed down the country lanes, the head lights shining through the darkness. Jeff was angry, and was driving like an idiot. He was thirty-two with brown hair and hazel eyes he was a thin man, and of medium height and build.

Monaca sat beside him chewing on gum, and clenching her teeth. She was a coloured woman with curly short hair, and a finely sculptured face. She was slim and athletic looking. All this because she had to get up early tomorrow for work.

They had been at a friend's party, and she had to leave it was getting late. But Jeff had been drinking with his buddies, and wanted to stay the night. But she really did have to get back even if he was half drunk.

They had been going out for five years now, and lived together, but he had never popped the question to her. Maybe it was time to leave him she thought as she looked at his angry face. There was a loud bang and the car swerved wildly, and came off the road. Jeff managed to brake, and the car hit the trunk of a tree, but not very hard.

"Well done Jeff you and your moods," Monaca said.

"Oh, shut up we are okay," he hissed.

"God you are such a baby sometimes," she cursed at him.

He smiled and winked at her then was out of the car.

She got out too, "What is it," she asked him.

"The damn tyre has blown," he said scratching his head.

"Well put on the spare," she said.

"I would only we don't have one," he said and shrugged.

She cursed him under her breath.

"Come on there is a house over there," he said pointing.

Monaca could see lights through the trees.

"Okay," she said following him.

The house was big and old looking with a long winding drive way. They walked up the gravel drive, and up to the strong looking front door. There was the head of a demon for a door knocker, and it seemed to hiss at them as they knocked.

The door was opened by a large man with a bald head and glasses. He was huge and towered over the couple he wore a tatty dark suit. Jeff looked at Monaca then again at the large man in front of them.

"We had a crash on the road can we use your phone please," Jeff asked in a kind voice.

"Come in then," the man said in a deep voice, and showed them inside.

They stood in the large hallway a flight of stairs going up in front of them. The inside was gloomy, and all the blinds over the windows were pulled down.

"Nice place," Jeff said with a whistle.

"The man of the house will be down shortly," the big man said, and led them into a dining room.

Pictures adorned the walls and a large table with twelve chairs stood in the centre. There was a sofa to one side, and the couple sat down and waited.

"This is some place darling," Jeff said nudging her.

She smiled she really had enough of Jeff this night.

Then the door opened and a tall handsome man stood before them. He was dressed in black save for the white lacy shirt. He had a pale face and red lips, and green eyes that seemed to look into your very soul.

"Welcome to my house I am count Van Garth," he bowed to them.

"This is some house count I am Jeff and this is my girlfriend Monaca," Jeff said taking the man's cold hand in his.

Then the count turned to Monaca, and smiled his face lit up and he studied her beauty.

"Very pleased to meet you my dear," he said.

"Thank you count," she replied.

Monaca found herself blushing he was so handsome. He seemed to be stripping her clothes off her with his eyes, and it turned her on.

"You met my butler Garrison," said the count.

"Yes, what a big guy he is," Jeff replied.

The count laughed, but kept his eyes on Monaca.

"I'm afraid I have no phone here, but please stay for dinner Garrison makes a lovely meal," he bowed again to them.

Jeff looked at Monaca, and she nodded her head yes.

The meal was lovely steak and kidney pie, and mash with vegetables. They ate in silence the count watching them from the head of the table. The count did not eat, and played with a glass of wine. They sat on either side of him, and Garrison disappeared once the meal was served.

"Damn that was lovely now I need the toilet now," Jeff said and laughed.

"Up stairs second on the right," the count said.

He watched as Jeff went out of the room.

"I would so like to talk with you my dear, but that will have to wait," the count smiled at her.

She smiled back, "Why is that count."

"I must leave you for a moment, but I will be back shortly," he stood and bowed to her.

"No problem count," she smiled at him.

Jeff found the toilet it was a large room, and had a bath and shower inside to. He lifted the lid, and began to urinate into the toilet bowl. He heard a noise behind him, and looked in the large mirror there was no one there. He carried on and sighed damn he needed that.

All that drink inside his belly he thought. He done up his jeans, and was going to turn when something grabbed him from behind. It was strong, and he could not move in its grip. A hand went over his mouth, and then he felt sharp teeth sink into his neck. At first it was painful as hell, but then he became dozy, and it did not feel so bad after all.

The man's body fell to its knees, and the count twisted off its head. He did not want the man changing.

He looked at the head in his hands and smiled at it, "Now Monaca is all mine, Jeff."

"My dear Monaca Jeff is not well, and has been taken to a spare room please will you join him," the count said.

He had come back into the room, and he looked redder in the face flushed, and healthy looking.

"Oh, dear I knew he drank too much," Monaca said and left the room following the count upstairs.

The room was empty as she entered, and she heard the lock of the door. The large bed was made but unused there was a bedside cabinet, and a chest of draws.

"Where is Jeff," she said turning to the count.

He looked at her with his green eyes and she melted.

"My dear you are so beautiful and deserve to stay that way forever, join me my dear in eternal love."

"I know what you are," she said lying on the bed.

"Yes, my dear," he said he had allowed her to see some of his life.

He cuddled up next to her on the bed, and felt her breasts against him as she breathed. He kissed her on the mouth, and her tongue went into his. He rubbed her breasts, and she moaned in delight. He massaged her bottom, and ran his hand over her tight jeans. She rubbed at his crotch, but she could feel no erection.

Then he sank his teeth into her neck, and she cried out in pain. Then she felt herself drifting away on a sea of love and pleasure.

"Come back to me my dear," he said he was leaning over her.

She smiled up at his face and said, "Yes my love."

Garrison came into the room holding a tray the big man looked at the two at the table. There was a storm raging outside, and the room kept lighting up with the lightening flashes.

"What a gorgeous evening my love," the count said.

Garrison put the tray down, and gave the two a glass of red wine each.

"What a great vintage," the count said looking at the wine glass in his hand.

"I think this was last year at the country dance," Garrison said.

The counts face lit up and he smiled, "Yes Garrison you are right that young girl I took."

Monaca sniffed the wine and smiled, "Smells wonderful my love," she said and smiled at the count.

She looked at the portraits around the room so many, and they all looked alike.

"My family has been around for century's my dear," the count said reading her mind.

Garrison was a happy man it had been so long now.

The count had been on his own for so long.

But now he had a madam as well to look after, and that pleased him.

"Enjoy sir and madam," Garrison said and left the room.

"Too a new beginning," said the count rising his glass.

"To us," Monaca said smiling.

The end

C Robert Paul Bennett 2016

3

The blood gang

The five bikes roared down the street of the city, and people looked away. They were the notorious blood gang, and they wore the words proudly on their leather jackets. The police knew about them of course, but they mainly left them alone.

The gang owned this side of the city, and they kept their turf clean. Any other gang would wind up hurt badly, and the police would turn a blind eye. At least the gang mainly only ever hit outside gangs, and kept the neighbourhood clean.

Darren Grim was twenty-four and leader of the blood gang, he had short dark hair and a goatee beard. He was tall and thin, and liked to show off his tattoos on his arms and chest. He was called grim because he always looked on the grim side of things.

Ricky Dirt was twenty-three with short blonde hair and a tanned face. He was also tall and thin, and was called dirt because he looked dirty.

Bryan pusher was twenty-five with short curly brown hair he had a spotty face, and kind of ugly. He looked like a monkey and was short and fat he was called pusher because he sold drugs to the school kids.

Percy beak was twenty-four with short brown hair, and a bony face and a large nose. He was short and thin, and called beak because of his nose.

Shawn corky was the oldest at twenty-six he had short ginger hair, and was covered in tattoos. He was board shouldered and large in frame, he was called corky because he loved his wine. He never drank wine that did not have a cork.

It was early evening, and almost turning dark as the gang rode onwards.

The bikes turned into an alley way, and speed down at top speed. They saw the man up ahead they had been tipped off that there was a man selling drugs on their turf. The young boy with the man run off, but the man stayed as the bikers got off their bikes.

The man was tall and thin with a handsome face, and dark clothes.

"Hey man you don't sell that shit on our turf," grim said smacking his fist into the palm of his other hand.

The tall man shrugged, "Didn't know this was your turf."

"Well, it is buster," dirt said leaning on his bike.

"What shall we do with him guys," grim said smiling at his gang.

"Give him a damned good kicking," pusher said.

"That's only for starters," beak said scratching his long nose.

"Come on let's not talk about it lets do it," corky said, and marched towards the man.

They kicked the man senseless he did not stand a chance.

The gang stood over the bleeding body panting, "That's enough lads he has learnt his lesson," grim panted.

"Fucker," dirt hissed panting.

"Right dirt you get rid of the body fast just dumps him somewhere else off our turf," grim said.

"Okay grim," dirt said.

He watched as the other four bikers rode off.

Dirt knew that they never left beaten bodies on their turf they kept the streets clean. Plus, they did not want the police sniffing around, no better to dump the body in another part of the city. Dirt turned, and looked down at the beaten man something was wrong.

He rubbed his tanned face, and could not figure out what it was. Then it came to him the man looked unharmed there was no blood, and then he smiled up at dirt.

"What the fuck," dirt said and stared as the man rose to his feet.

"I like you and I like your gang," the man said.

Then he was on dirt in a flash, and dirt felt pain as the man sank his teeth into his exposed throat. Dirt moaned in pain, and then ecstasy, and then the world went blank.

Grim sighed and sipped his beer from the bottle it was the next evening. He was with pusher, and they sat on a grave in the local graveyard. They often came here to chill out it was quiet and prefect.

"Wonder where the dick dirt is," pusher said drinking his beer.

"Fuck knows, but at least the body is gone so he done something right," grim laughed.

"I second that," pusher said laughing.

"I third that," a voice called out.

"Who is that," pusher said looking into the dark.

"Is that you dirt," grim asked.

Dirt came into the moon light, and smiled at his friends.

"You wouldn't believe what happened to me," he said smiling he looked so pale.

"Tell us," Grim said.

"Oh, I can do better than that," dirt smiled.

"What do you mean," pusher asked.

"I can show you," and dirt's eyes turned red, and he leapt at them full of hunger.

Beak and corky had been to a party that night, and were pretty pissed. They had begun to walk home when they started to hear noises coming from alley ways. It began as owl hoots and then moved onto wolf howling. Who was trying to scare them?

It was the rest of the gang of course, and the two men smiled. Corky would show them when they came out the gang knew not to mess with him.

"Hey corky and beak come down here," a voice called from down an alley way.

It started to rain, and the two men entered the alley.

"Where the fucks are they," corky asked.

Then a face suddenly came out of the dark and said loudly, "Boo."

It was grim, but he looked pale and ill both men jumped.

"Hey cut that shit out man," corky said his heart racing.

Then corky heard from next to him, "Oh it's you," said beak.

But when corky looked at this side beak had gone.

"Don't worry he is only up there," grim said pointing upwards.

Dirt was floating in the air carrying beak in his arms.

"What the fuck is going on," corky said.

"Hey let me down," shouted beak.

"Oh okay," dirt said and let him go, he crashed to the earth, and lay still but moaning.

"What the fuck are you doing," corky said his eyes wide.

"We will show you my friend," grim said.

Then pusher, dirt and grim were on top of him, and after they finished with corky, they went for beak.

The gang rode the next night, and stopped by an alley. They could see a young couple kissing.

"I'm as hungry as hell," corky said.

"Yes, me too I fancy a feast," pusher said.

"Come on then gang," grim said, and they parked their bikes.

"Carol, I love you so much," Drake said smiling at the girl he was feeling as horny as hell.

"I love you too Drake," she said rubbing his hair.

Carol was a slight girl with long blonde hair she looked too thin like a model. Drake was tall and thin with spots on his handsome face.

"I love you too Drake," grim said from behind him.

"Hey who is that," Drake said, but was taken by strong arms.

They held him, and grim got the girl in his embrace.

He kissed her hard on the lips, "Man she is a shit kisser," he said.

"Leave her alone you brutes," Drake moaned.

"Or you will do what," grim said holding the girl.

She seemed in a daze, and let the man do anything.

Grim rubbed her small breasts, "Not much there," he said smiling.

"You bastard," Drake moaned.

"Hey you hold your tongue young man," pusher said.

"Yes, or we will rip it out and eat it," dirt said with a smile.

"Does she have any hair down below," grim asked Drake.

"What," he said in horror.

"It's a simple question does she have hair below," he said looking at Drake.

"I don't know," Drake moaned.

"Then let's find out," grim said and lifted her skirt, and pulled down her panties.

"There she has," he said smiling at the small bush of brown hair.

Pusher put his hand over the boy's mouth as he was about to scream.

"Corky you and me, the rest take him," grim said in a stern voice the games were over.

Grim and corky took the young girl, and the rest took the young boy, it was over quickly.

They beheaded the bodies, and put them into the trash bins there would be no new members.

They rode the next night and felt strong like they were top of the food chain. Nothing could stop them, and they wanted the whole city. They were riding to a part of the city no one liked after dark.

The gang that owned this turf were meant to be fierce, and no one crossed them. The gang would teach the fierce gang a lesson this was going to be so much fun. They rode into the part of the city the houses were run down, and the place was in darkness.

A few street lights lit the place, but it looked grim and foreboding. There were no people on the streets, and the gang rode down an alley way and stopped. They got off their bikes, and stood in the middle of the alley. There was a street light, but it only threw off a slight light, it was dim and gloomy.

"Hey fuckers we are taking this part of the city," grim shouted.

Then a jacket was thrown out, and landed in a puddle.

"What's that," dirt asked.

"It's a jacket jerk off," corky said.

Grim went to the jacket and picked it up the words 'night beasts' on the back.

"Okay night beasts we are taking over," grim shouted.

There was no reply.

"If you want to settle this, come out and face us," grim called out.

"This is going to be fun," beak said smiling.

"Damn right it is," pusher smiled.

Then all hell broke loose.

The dogs came at them from all sides, but no they were not dogs at all.

The vampires were strong, but so were the wolves. Corky had a wolf in his massive arms and he twisted, and the wolf's neck broke. But he was attacked by another, and pushed to the ground. Dirt and pusher fought side by side, and hit and kicked the wolves.

Grim was swatted aside like a fly, and set upon by two wolves. Beak tried to run, but was brought down by a pack of wolves. He screamed as he was ripped apart by the pack, his blood splashing onto the walls of the alley. A small stream of blood run under the pack, and made its way to a drain.

"Get out of here," shouted grim.

He was hurt and bleeding.

The wolves backed off, and let the gang ride out. They left two dead wolves on the ground. As the gang reached their own turf their wounds were already healed.

"We lost beak man," corky said with no emotion.

"Fuck him he was weak," dirt said.

"I got to meet their leader tomorrow on our turf, no one touches him okay," grim said parking his bike.

The gang walked towards the crypt in the cemetery their new home.

"Okay boss what's going to happen," pusher asked.

Grim looked at the lightening sky line and shook his head, "No idea he whispered into my ear."

Grim waited in the alley alone it was dark and raining. Then he saw a huge wolf trotting down the alley towards him. The wolf stopped, and sniffed the air, and looked this way and that.

Then before grim's eyes the wolf changed into a man.

The man got up from his hands and knees, and smiled he was huge.

He was built like a brick shit house, and had a bushy dark beard and a mane of dark hair. His eyes were dark and cruel, and he smiled at grim, but it was a smile that said I can rip you apart. The man came up to grim he was naked, his skin was white and hairy, his penis long and limp.

"I'm Mason," the man said in a deep voice.

"Grim," the vampire shook the man's hand.

The man smiled, "I think it's safe to say we should stay apart from each other."

Grim nodded his head yes, "I think that would be for the best Mason."

"Good then we keep to our own sides of the city okay," the big man said.

"Yes, I agree we will stay away from you and you us," grim said and smiled.

"You know I like you vampires, and I'm sorry we killed one of your kinds," Mason said sadly.

"I'm sorry too for killing two of your kind," grim replied.

Mason laughed, "That's no worries we are many and you are few."

"There were a lot of you the other night," grim said looking worried.

"That was only a small pack," Mason smiled.

Then the big man laughed, and slapped grim on the back, "Don't worry son we both keep our side of the bargain, and things will be just fine."

"Yes sir," grim replied.

With that Mason got on his hands and knees, and changed into a wolf again and howled into the night.

Then grim saw him loop off into the night.

The end

C Robert Paul Bennett 2016

4

Tiddles

The house was in darkness as the man entered via the window.

The fools had left the window open, and to him it was a certain invitation. He had a small pen torch, and found himself in the living room. He saw the wall television, and the sky box, and DVD player.

The row of DVDs on the shelfs along the wall, the big sofa and arm chairs the small coffee table. It reminded him of a joke he had heard and he smiled.

'The burglar came into the living room and was about to pick up the television when a voice said, "Jesus is watching you."

The Burglar shone his pen light, and saw that it was a parrot on a perch.

The parrot repeated, "Jesus is watching you."

He laughed and said, "What's your name."

The bird replied, "I am Moses."

The burglar laughed and said, "What kind of family call their parrots Moses."

The bird replied, "The kind of family that call their Rottweiler Jesus."

The man smiled at the joke this was going to be an easy job. He had been looking at the house for days, and saw no one he was sure they were away. Then the light went on, and the burglar stood there, and looked at the man in the door way. He was caught red handed.

"Hey mister," was all he could say.

The burglar was a small thin man, and the man in the door way was huge. He wore all black with a white shirt, and his head was bald.

He had evil little eyes, and a large mouth which he was grinning with.

"I will have to set my dog on you now."

The burglar had vision of a huge killer dog and said, "No please mister I will just go."

"Sorry pal too late for that Tiddles come boy," the man called.

"Tiddles," the burglar repeated strange name for a big dog.

Then a small Yorkshire terrier appeared in the door way next to the large man.

"Is that your dog," the man laughed.

"Oh no you shouldn't have done that tiddles doesn't like being laughed at," said the huge man.

"Oh, fuck off," the burglar laughed, and slapped his thigh.

Then the small dog opened its mouth to reveal rows of sharp teeth. Its mouth seemed to open, and cover the rest of its head, the mouth was huge. The small dog leapt at the burglar and tore into his throat.

The man gasped, and tried to fight off the little dog, but it was too late his throat had been ripped open.

Blood splattered all over the room some covering the huge man's face, he licked his lips. The burglar lay dead, and the dog lapped up the puddles of blood.

"Now I'm going to have to clean this mess up," sighed the big man.

The big man walked through the park with his dog a few nights later. It was dark and the man sat down on a park bench all was normally quiet at this time. But he could see a man playing with his dog on the grass. The man owned a pit bull, and he was swinging it round by its lead. The pit bull had the lead in its mouth, and would not let go.

"Strong dog," the bald man called out.

The man who was thin and tall looked over at the man on the bench. The man was young maybe in his twenties, and smiled a cocky smile. The young man walked over, and looked at the small Yorkshire terrier.

"That thing would be my dog's dinner mate," the man laughed.

"Oh really, and why do you say that," the huge man replied.

"What's a big guy like you doing with a small dog like that," the young man laughed again.

"Because unlike you I don't have to pretend I got a big dick," the large man said with a smile.

"What do you mean by that," the young man asked.

Thick as well as ugly thought the huge man on the bench.

"I mean I don't go round showing off my dog, and thinking it makes me look like I got a big dick."

"You're fucked up mate," the young man said.

He looked down at the small dog in anger and added, "I should let my dog go, and he will eat that little shit."

"Be my guest tiddles would like a game with your dog," the man on the bench said.

"Game my dog will rip it apart."

"So go on let your dog go," said the men dropping his dog's lead.

"Right, you asked for this mate," the man let his dog go.

Tiddles ran off into the bushes, and the pit bull followed.

"Kill the cunt Tyson," the man shouted.

Then they heard whimpering pitiful whimpering, and then it went silent. The man looked at the big man on the bench, "That sounded like my dog," he said in debrief.

"Yes, I believe it was," the man laughed.

Then the man on the bench was upon him, and the man cried out as fangs pieced his neck. The huge man drained the body, and went into the bushes. He buried both the man and the dog in a shallow grave, and picked up his dog's lead.

"Come on tiddles lets go home."

The small boy was sobbing and walking aimlessly around he was in an alley way.

The huge man saw the boy crying, and walked towards him. The boy was maybe ten with short brown hair, and a dimple in his chin. He wore shorts and a t-shirt, and trainers on his feet. The boy gasped when he saw the huge man, and backed away in fear.

"Hey kid its okay," said the big man, and let his dog go.

The dog went up to the boy, and the boy bent down. The dog licked the boys face, and the boy laughed as the dog let him play with it. The dog ran round the boy, and the boy tried to catch it. The boy was now laughing, and he looked at the big man.

"Your dog is so cool mister."

"Good now take my hand, and let's get you home," said the big man.

"Can I walk your dog," the boy asked.

"Of course, you can his name is tiddles," the big man gave the small boy the lead.

The boy took his hand, and they all walked off.

They soon found the boys home, and the man watched from a distance as the boy rang the bell. His mother swept him up in her arms, and she was sobbing with delight. The father came and kissed his son so glad to see him.

The big man smiled, "Come on tiddles lets go home."

The big man walked the dark streets with his dog, and looked up at the full moon. It looked so eerie with clouds moving across it. He heard a noise coming from a house nearby, and went to investigate. He looked in through a front window, and saw a man beating his wife.

"You fucking cunt," the man hissed as he hit his wife again.

She fell to the floor out cold, blood running from her mouth. She was a cute looking woman with blonde hair, and a pretty looking face. The man was tall, and thin and ugly.

The big man marched round the back, and kicked in the back door. The thin man looked at him standing there in the back door frame.

His eyes went wide with fear.

"Who the fuck are you," the man said in fear.

"Get him tiddles," the huge man said.

Then the thin man saw the dog and laughed, "That thing don't make me laugh," the thin man said.

But he did not laugh for long as the dog unhooked its jaw, and opened its mouth wide like a snake. The man screamed as his throat was ripped open, and the dog fed on the dead corpse. The big man cleaned up the place as best he could, and then dumped the body in some bins close by. He did not really care if the police found the bodies, and there was still blood splattered around the kitchen.

"Come on tiddles lets go home."

That night the man cuddled up with the dog in his coffin. There was plenty of room for both, now it was time to sleep.

He stroked the dog and said, "What tiddles likes I like, and what tiddles doesn't like I don't like."

He kissed his dog, and closed his eyes.

The end

C Robert Paul Bennett 2016

5

Vampire leeches

Matt was excited, and walked along the stream looking for the best possible shot. The countryside was breath taking, and the documentary was going well. It was all about the countryside and Matt was going to make a killing with this. He was sure it was going to be a huge hit on the television. The camera men were getting ready, and Matt stepped into the stream.

It was not deep, and he waded into the water in his jeans, he thought it looked better than wearing wellingtons. He breathed in the English country air and smiled, maybe after all this he would move here.

He felt a sharp pain in his leg and then another, 'what the fuck' he thought.

More pain shot through his body and he cried out, "Hey guys will you help me for a second."

The camera men pulled him out of the stream, and Matt collapsed onto the ground moaning. His jeans were moving as if something were underneath them. They rolled up his jeans, and saw long black leeches clinging to his skin.

One man began to pull them off, "Hey don't do that might infect him," said a small man with curly brown hair and glasses.

They called an ambulance, and waited Matt did not look good at all, and he kept on moaning.

David and Alan were playing by the stream and Alan bent down and said, "Look at this worm," the boy said.

Alan was wearing shorts and a t-shirt that read, 'I rule ok.'

He had short blonde hair and blue eyes set in a cute looking face. David was a plumper boy with a round chubby face, and short brown hair. He too wore shorts and a t-shirt with the words, 'so do I.'

"That's not a worm," David said and picked up the long black thing from the stream.

"Look there's loads of them," Alan said pointing.

Sure, enough the long black shapes were swimming towards the two boys at speed.

"Shit," David cried out holding up his hand, "The thing got me."

He shook his hand, but the thing would not come off, Alan moved to help him, and slipped on the bank. He rolled into the stream and sat up in the water as the black shapes descended on him.

David was in the water trying to help his screaming friend the things were all over him, and sticking like glue. They were attaching themselves to him as well, and he began to feel faint.

David stopped helping his friend and fell face first into the stream, Alan had stopped screaming.

The next day Thomas stood staring at the small stream and thought, 'what the hell is going on here.'

He was the sergeant on duty today, and so this would be his case now. This was only a small town, and two dead boys did not happen very often.

"I found them this morning officer I was walking my dog," said a man talking with one of his constables.

The man was maybe in his fifties with grey hair and horn-rimmed glasses. Thomas sighed the bodies had been in a bad state as well, like they had been drained of blood. The bodies also had black marks on the skin, and he shivered as he recalled seeing them for the first time.

"Tony, you stay here and take his man's statement I will be back shortly," he said to the constable talking to the dog man.

"Okay boss," Tony replied.

Tony was a good man, and Thomas liked him he was tall and thin with blonde hair. Unlike Thomas who was short and fat with dark hair and olive skin, from his mother's Spanish side. He began to walk away, and stopped a tall thin man was looking at him.

"Can I help you sir," Thomas asked the man.

The man looked nervous, and was looking at the stream.

"I'm Matt," the man said looking away from the stream to Thomas.

He was tall and thin with receding brown hair, but he had a handsome face.

"I was attacked here a few weeks ago by leeches," Matt told the officer.

"Really Matt I'm Thomas I'm in charge here," he said and shook the man's hand.

"Yes, I almost died of blood loss I was lucky," Matt said again looking at the stream.

"What happened Thomas?"

Thomas sighed and rubbed his chin, "Two boys killed looks like they were drained."

"My god," Matt said looking Thomas in the eyes.

"Where will you be staying Matt," Thomas asked him.

"The hotel in town I can help you with this Thomas, I want these vampires killed."

"I might need all the help I can get on this one Matt vampire's you say."

"Yes, they nearly drained me, and they killed these two boys the same way."

"Let's talk about this later," Thomas said moving Matt away from the scene.

He had just seen the local reporter with his note book and wanted to avoid him.

The hotel room was small bit cosy, and Matt lay on the double bed. The room had a cabinet and a chest of draws and a small wardrobe, there was no bathroom you had to share one down the hall.

Matt closed his eyes, and breathed deeply he was tired. He dreamed of leeches and he was running through a sewer, and the smell was awful.

He had never seen so much shit in one place, and it was splashing up at him as he ran. He ran in slow motion, and when he looked down the water had turned into jelly.

He looked behind and saw the leeches closing in on him, and screamed out loud. An old woman was at the side of the sewer tunnel, and she put her finger to her lips. He could not run any farther and stopped and turned round they were almost on him. He turned, and something big and black blocked out the tunnel in front of him, and he screamed.

Matt opened his eyes and sighed, "Thank fuck that was only a dream," he said to himself.

Matt sat in Thomas office it was small and tidy, pictures of Thomas fishing were on the walls. He was holding a long pike in one of them, a good catch.

"So, Matt tell me what happened to you," Thomas wanted as much information as possible.

Matt told Thomas about that day, and the making of the television documentary.

Thomas sighed after he had finished, "The two boys were drained of blood by an animal or insect unknown."

"Unknown, but they are leeches," Matt said.

"I was told the lab could not identify the bite marks so we are dealing with a new breed of leeches Matt."

"Holy damn," Matt said.

"Holy damn indeed Matt we need to sort this out now."

"I'm all for that Thomas."

"Good come on let's go back to that stream."

They went back to the stream later that day, but they found nothing.

No sign of any leeches at all the stream was clear and they searched downstream, but still nothing.

They gave up after an hour it had started to rain.

Sam had worked in the sewers all his life, and he liked his job it paid him well, and he got used to the smell and the rats. He was sixty with a bald head and glasses on a plump round face he was well over weight, but did not give a damn. He was looking forward to retiring with his wife Rita, and would travel the world with her.

He walked down a tunnel, and shone his flash light he had not been down this part before. It had been many years since the town's sewer system had been checked. The walls looked good, and the water was running well all looked good to him. Then he saw a black shape in the water, and shone his flash light at it, it was a leech.

"Fucking things," he cursed, and kicked at the leech.

Then he saw more and they came at him, he kicked at them, and the water splashed over the walls. One attached itself to his cheek and he tried to pull it off, but it was stuck fast. Leeches went into his wellingtons, and he cried out in pain as they attached himself to his bare skin.

Thomas smiled at Matt and said, "How do you like my new toy," he held up the flame thrower.

"Wow that looks the business where did you get it from," Matt asked him.

"I have a friend in the army he owes me a favour," Thomas said smiling.

"That should get the bastards," Matt smiled.

They were standing outside the sewer grate the water ran into the stream.

"Sam Jenkins didn't show up after work yesterday he was working in here," Thomas said nodding his head into the sewer.

"Another one dead," Matt replied.

"I was on the internet last night this won't be the first outbreak of leeches."

"Really Thomas do tell."

"Few years ago, a small town had a similar problem, and they burnt them out that's why I got the flame thrower."

The two men wadded into the stream of water in the sewer they both wore wellingtons. Matt was scared of course they had almost killed him once. Thomas was more open minded as he had yet to see the leeches. As they turned into another tunnel the water began to get dirty and smelly.

"This is a waste tunnel the water that runs into the stream is clean," Thomas said.

"I was wondering about that," Matt said.

Half an hour later, and nothing not a sign.

"This is a waste of time there is nothing here," Thomas said shining his torch.

"Hang on look over there," Matt said pointing.

They saw three leeches swimming towards them.

"My god," said Thomas.

Matt took out a metal bar, and began to beat at the leeches.

"Good work they weren't so bad," Thomas said looking down at the dead and battered leeches.

"No but they are," Matt said pointing.

An army of black leeches swam towards them there were thousands of the things. They were moving through the dirty water, and over each other in their eagerness to reach the two men.

The two men moved quickly running through the dirty water. As they rounded a bend they stopped, and looked down a side tunnel. There was something big and black, and it stared at them with beady evil eyes. The torch light picked up its dense matted fur and its long tail.

Then the men were running onwards.

They came out of the sewer, and ran up to the car panting.

"Come on get in," said Thomas throwing the flame thrower in the back.

"What the hell was that thing," Matt said gasping for air.

"Hell, if I know," Thomas replied.

Thomas parked the car by a petrol pump, and went into the garage at the side of the road. Matt stood outside as Thomas talked to the man inside, Matt saw him show the man his badge. Thomas came out smiling, and took hold of a petrol pump, and motioned Matt to follow him.

There was a drain cover near the petrol garage, and the two men lifted it up.

"This leads down to where we were," Thomas said smiling.

"When we were down there, I saw this cover and smelt petrol," he said with a grin.

"Okay now I'm with you Thomas," Matt said grinning.

Thomas pulled on the pump and petrol went down into the sewer.

"This will run back into the stream," Thomas said after a few minutes.

He put the pump back, and the two men got back into the car and drove off.

At the other side the two men saw the petrol running into the water of the stream. They also saw a group of leeches swimming idly about.

"Let's torch these bastards Thomas," Matt grinned.

The small man smiled and took out a lighter, and walked to the side of the bank. The leeches were swimming around in circles looking for food no doubt.

"Where do you think they came from," Matt asked the small round policeman.

Thomas shrugged, "Like I said a read a report on the net, but they were just there no origin."

Thomas added, "But that other thing scares me that was a big son of a bitch."

Matt shivered at the thought.

Thomas flicked the Zippo, and threw it into the water.

It was a chain reaction the water ignited, and then the flames went into the sewer tunnel, and then a series of explosions happened. They saw a drain cover fly into the air, and a pillow of smoke rising.

"That's got the fuckers," Matt said punching the air.

"I sure hope so," Thomas replied.

The end

C Robert Paul Bennett 2016

6

Youth bathing

Barry sat at the dining table eating his breakfast which was a bowl of corn flakes. His parents sat with him before both would go to work, and him to school. Barry was almost sixteen, and was staying at school an extra year acting as a senior boy.

That gave him the right to boss the smaller kids around for a year, and study before going to college. He was a handsome boy with brown short hair, and the makings of a small moustache on his lip.

He was of medium height and skinny, he loved to play football, and that is what he wanted to be a professional footballer. But his dream was hard he had already failed trails at his local semi professional team. But he would not give up on his dream.

"They found a tramp dead yesterday," his father said reading the morning paper.

He was a tall man with a bald head and glasses he looked like a book worm. Which in a way he was as he worked for a publishing company in the city.

This mother worked part time on a building site making the breakfasts for the hungry men. She had curly ginger hair and freckles on her cute face she had a good body, and Barry would sometimes look at her.

He was getting sexually inquisitive now.

"Really poor man," his mother replied.

His father just nodded, and carried on reading the paper.

"We got new neighbours," his mother said.

"Really that's nice dear," his father said taking no interest.

Then Barry saw his best friend Andrew standing in the door way.

"Okay got to go Andrews here," he said and kissed both parents on their cheeks.

Andrew was the same height and build as Barry, and he had dark long hair, and was also a handsome boy.

They walked off together talking about football.

Barry was in the back garden that evening putting out the rubbish for his mother. They had a small back garden with a shed, and the bins at the bottom by the wooden fence. As he turned away from the bins, he saw the most beautiful and stunning woman he had ever seen in his short life. She was in the garden next door. She was tall and slim with large breasts, and long flowing red hair. She wore red lip stick, and dark eye shadow. Her face was finely sculptured.

She saw him and he tried to hide, "Hey young man do want some lemonade its home made," she said to him.

"It's okay I'm Lena and I won't bite," she added smiling.

He breathed deeply and found his voice, "Thank you."

He leaned on the oven in the kitchen, and drank his lemonade it tasted wonderful.

He saw a man an ape of a man with huge strong arms, and a barrel chest. He was short, but very stocky and looked like he could rip your arms off.

"That's Barny my helper," she said smiling at Barry.

He drank his lemonade and eyed her body up and down when he went home, he had an erection.

Barry was naked, and standing before the woman Lena, she had her eyes closed, and was waiting for him to take her. She was even more beautiful naked. She had large round breasts with nipples that stuck upwards. She had a flat belly and a triangle of curly red pubic hair between her legs. He almost fell on top of her.

He entered her and moaned in pleasure it felt so good, and he moved inside her quickly. He could not hold back and fired his semen inside her, and woke up in a sweat. He felt his boxer shorts he had shot his load inside his boxers that was the first time he had ever had a wet dream.

That evening Barry could not contain himself any longer he wanted the woman Lena badly. He saw that her back door was open, and sneaked into her garden. He listened all was quiet, and he went inside the kitchen. He crept up the stairs in the half light, the landing light was on.

Then he was at the bedroom door, and he slowly pushed it inwards, and stared into the room. There was an old hag on the bed looking at him.

Her face was so wrinkled it looked like a road map she had long white hair, and wore a night gown. She eyed him with evil little eyes, she somehow looked familiar.

"Who are you young man," she asked in a crackling voice like an old witch.

"I'm sorry madam I was looking for Lena," he said standing there.

"Lena is out I'm her mother," but the old woman never gave her name.

"I'm sorry," he said once more and closed the door, and walked away.

Barry was keeping an eye on the house next door, and he saw Barny enter with another man late at night. It was the weekend so Barry did not need to go to bed early, he watched horror movies on the horror channel. He kept going to the window and looking.

Then in the early hours of the morning he saw barny again this time carrying a large plastic bag over his shoulder. Barny put the plastic bag in the boot of his car, and drove off.

Barry did not see the other man come out of the house.

The next day he saw Lena in the garden the day was over cast, and there was rain in the air. He was digging his mothers flower beds so she could start to grow her flowers for the summer.

"Barry, do you want some lemonade," Lena called to him.

He almost dropped the spade he was holding, and gulped she looked awesome. She was wearing tight shorts and a tight t-shirt that showed her large nipples off. He stood in the kitchen drinking his lemonade, and she smiled at him.

"I bet you are a big young boy yes," she said and eyed him up those eyes looked so familiar.

He saw her looking at his erection in his shorts, and went red in the face. She smiled at him and took his hand in hers, "Come with me my lover boy."

They made love five times Barry just could not stop, but finally he could do no more. It was wonderful and when they heard Barny come back she ushered him out.

Barry packed his bags the next night he was going to run away with Lena. He had not told her yet, but he knew she would go with him. He would find work somewhere, and they could rent an apartment. It would be just so great. He packed his case and smiled he had never been in love before, and it felt wonderful to him.

Lena leaned back in the bath, and rubbed the red fluid all over her body and face. It felt so good, and she could feel the wrinkles vanishing. A dead man was on the floor by the bath naked and drained of all his blood. Barny always did such a good job in finding blood donors for her.

She was an ancient vampire born into the darkness many centuries ago. She went from town to town, and city to city never staying too long. She enjoyed sex with men, and the young boy's energy excited her. She would stay a little longer the young men excited her so much.

She splashed blood over her face and swallowed some of it, it tasted so good. But she did not need to feed on blood only to bath in it to keep herself young and gorgeous.

He went into her house by the back way, and went up the stairs carrying his suit case.

Lena was naked on her bed and she smiled at him, "Come to me lover boy," she said in a sexy voice.

He slipped his clothes off and she eyed the suit case, "What's that for my love."

"I want to run away with you Lena," he said getting into bed.

She smiled, "Maybe tomorrow," she said and began to kiss and grope him.

Barry was at the back door again the following night he had left his suit case in Lena's room. Sure, that tonight they would run away together, and live happily ever after. He made his way up the stairs, and saw barny in the living room watching the television. The man made no sign to show that he had seen Barry.

Barry slipped up the stairs he was already hard, and could not wait to make love to Lena. He paused outside her bedroom door something was different, a different smell. Like old people, and moth balls.

He slowly pushed open the door, and saw the old hag on the bed again. Why did the old hag sleep in Lena's bed?

He stared at her, and she stared back she was so familiar.

"Is Lena here," he asked standing there, and feeling stupid.

He saw his case sitting by the side of the bed.

The old woman looked at him and replied, "No Lena has gone away."

"Gone away but we were going away together," he said suddenly shocked, and disappointed.

The old woman laughed like a witch and said, "Go away with you."

Then Barry had a bad feeling that someone was behind him, and he turned round slowly. But something hit him from behind, and the world went blank. Barny dragged the boy into the bath room, and hung him upside down like a piece of meat.

He cut the boys throat, and let his blood run into the bath tub and then went back to the bedroom.

"Is my bath ready Barny," she said as he helped her out of the bed.

"Yes, my dear it's nearly run for you," he replied.

"Good I have that young boy Andrew coming round soon."

The end

C Robert Paul Bennett 2016

7

Bats

It was a cold and windy night, and the farmer pulled his coat up around his neck. His wife was still in bed snoring her head off, he smiled after all these years he still love her dearly. He had been woken up by his cows crying. That is the only way he could describe the noise they made. It puzzled him greatly something must be attacking them.

He made sure the shot gun was loaded and ready to use, and stepped out into the night shining his flash light. He was a short stocky man from years of working the land. He walked over to the field and stopped, and shone his light. There were maybe two or three cows on the ground.

One was standing up making whining noise he shone his light at the cow. It was covered in something, and he climbed over the wooden fence and got nearer. The things were black, and moving over the cow's body. He cursed as he suddenly realised what they were, "Bloody bats I be god damned," he hissed.

Then the bats took off into the air and he followed them with his flash light. They circled in the air, and then came back down.

"Fuck," he cursed as they came right for him. He tripped in his panic, and dropped both the gun and flash light.

Arthur looked at the sigh it was a bloody mess, four dead cows, and a dead man to boot. He was looking forward to a weekend away with his girlfriend, but this would put paid to that. He was on slender hooks with her anyway he never spent enough time with her. His job as a policeman took up all his time.

'Why don't you marry the bloody police force' was her favourite saying.

He was thirty-eight and was looking for promotion, and so had to work hard. He was of medium height with short brown hair, and acnes scars on his face. He had suffered badly as a teenager. They had found dead bats at the scene as well 'bloody bats' he thought. They had been sent to the lab.

The farmer's wife was no help she had slept through the whole thing. A shot gun and flash light lay on the ground, the gun not been fired.

The bodies had been drained of blood, and he shivered at the thought of vampire bats on the loose.

A few days later Arthur got a call from the lab it was Joyce on the other end of the line. He liked Joyce she was slim and good looking with large breasts, and a happy face.

"So, what you got for me Joyce," he said into the phone.

"Not much I'm afraid the bats are vampire bats, and they seem to be normal."

"Normal they sucked a man and four cows dry they don't normally do that now do they," he sighed it was no good getting angry with Joyce.

"No, they don't maybe sometimes they suck animal's blood, but they don't drain, and attack in large numbers."

He heard her sigh down the line then she added, "I can only guess that something is making them aggressive, and changing their behaviour."

"Well thank you Joyce," he sighed and put down the phone. He was back to square one he had nothing on this case.

Derek sat in the garden it was a chilly evening, but relaxing. He had a can of beer in his hand, and he was watching the stars. He was sixty-nine, and enjoyed his retirement, lazy days, and lazy nights. He had a head of white hair, and a thick white bushy beard. Next to him was his wife Nora she was a big lady with curly grey hair and a fat piggish face.

"Nora go get me a sandwich," he asked her.

"Go get it yourself you lazy old bastard," she hit back at him.

"Come on you fat old cow do some work, and you wouldn't be so fat," he cursed at her.

They lived like this every day arguing.

"Well at least I don't look like I belong in a captain bird's eye television advert."

"Look you fat cow," he was going to say more, but stopped.

"What's that," he said pointing something was on the top of the fence looking at them.

It was small and furry, and had wings and evil little eyes.

"It's a rat," said his wife.

"Rats don't fly no it's a bat," he said getting up from his chair.

"Don't go to near it," she said uneasily.

Then they heard the beating of many wings in the sky, and then a black cloud came over them!

Derek was covered in bats, and he was beating at them wildly with his arms, and kicking out with his legs. Nora was crawling on the ground moaning her body also covered.

She fell face first onto the grass, and the hungry bats fed on her. Derek finally gave up the fight, and fell to the ground on his knees, and then toppled over.

Arthur scratched his head of brown hair, and sighed another scene from hell. The back garden was a mess again with dead bats, and dead people. The old couple not stood a chance he looked out over the garden fence, and saw the mountains.

"Hey Clive those mountains have they got caves," he said to his constable.

The young man Clive looked at Arthur, and then at the mountains.

He was tall and thin and had a boyish handsome face, "Yes sir we used to play in them as kids," Clive said smiling.

"Some of them are deep," Arthur asked.

"Yes, sir some we wouldn't go into," replied the constable.

Arthur sighed and carried on looking at the mountains, caves indeed maybe he should check this out. Bats loved caves and, he would bet all his money that is where they were coming from.

Arthur parked his car and got out already he could see caves in the side of the mountain.

He took out his flash light and moved over to the mountain, it would be a long day, but he had to search. He could have called a constable to help, but he wanted all the glory. He would find the bats, and report them, and then it would be the job of the exterminators to get rid of them. He searched cave after cave, but most of them were short and did not go far in.

Then he found a large cave, and it went deep into the mountain. He entered the dark cave, and it was chilly inside. He walked deeper and then stopped, and aimed his flash light high and saw a bat hanging from the ceiling. The smell was strong here, and he saw a puddle of white fluid on the ground.

"Bat shit," he said softly.

He shone his light, and saw thousands of them hanging from the ceiling!

He stood rooted to the spot what if he moved suddenly would they attack him. He had a vision of being covered in bats, and them biting at his skin, draining his blood. He shivered and back slowly away now he had to get the hell out, and report these bastard things.

Then he stopped and stared was that a man he saw, the dark shape was walking towards him. The shape stopped, and Arthur shone his torch at the man. It was indeed a man, and he wore all black, and his face was so pale.

"Hey mister we need to get the hell out of here," Arthur whispered to the man in black.

The man just stood there looking at Arthur, he shone his torch again at the man. He was tall and thin with a head of dark hair which was long, and tied back in a pony tail.

Then the man's eyes turned red, and Arthur almost dropped the torch.

Arthur cursed out loud, "Fuck it," but managed to compose himself. It must have been a trick of the light.

It was like when you took pictures with a camera, and got red eye on everyone. A trick of the light, and Arthur shone the torch back at the man. His eyes were still red, and he was still staring at Arthur. With his heart racing in his chest Arthur began to move backwards very slowly. This man was weird, and he wanted out of here.

Then the man threw his arms out wide and said in a clear and loud voice, "My Babies."

The bats began to move their wings, and come out of their sleep. Arthur paused, and the man laughed at him.

"My babies get him," the man shouted out.

The bats came down from the ceiling as one and flew straight at Arthur, who just stood there and screamed.

The end

C Robert Paul Bennett 2016

8

A boy's life

Little Clyde was a lonely boy he did not have any friends in this new home. He had not even made any friends at his new school. He was a small cute boy with blonde hair, and blue eyes he was a little chubby, but in a cute way. He wore shorts and a t-shirt with Frankie says on the front. He was out playing now by himself.

They had moved to the countryside, and vast fields stretched away into the distance all around their house. He was throwing a ball into the air and catching it when he saw that he was being watched. It was getting dark now, and soon his mother would be calling him in.

Clyde waved to the other boy standing in the field. The other boy waved him over, and Clyde went. The other boy was taller and a little older than Clyde he had dark short hair, and pale skin. But his green eyes were alive, and swimming with energy.

"Hi Clyde my name is Marion," the boy held out his hand.

Clyde took the hand it was cold and said, "How did you know my name."

The boy laughed, "Because you look like a Clyde."

The two boys began to play ball, and after a while Marion stopped and looked to his left.

"Hey Clyde watch this," Marion called to him, and Clyde watched.

Marion was quick so quick that Clyde could not keep up with his movements. Then Marion was in front of him holding a rabbit. The rabbit's throat was torn open, and blood ran from Marion's mouth.

"Try its lovely," Marion said and Clyde put his mouth to the dead rabbit, and tasted its blood.

"Yuk that's disgusting," Clyde said wiping his mouth with the back of his hand.

Marion laughed, and threw the dead rabbit away.

The next evening the two boys played ball again, and they laughed, and rolled around in the grass.

Marion looked at Clyde and smiled, "I want to show you something amazing."

"Okay," Clyde replied.

Then Clyde was taken off his feet, and he was riding the air with Marion holding him tight around the waist.

"Wow this is so cool how can you fly," Clyde cried out in wonder.

"It's just something I can do," Marion replied.

They soared up into the clouds, and then swooped down close to the ground. Then up again, and then across the fields, and over the roofs of houses. When the ride was over Clyde stood panting, and trying to get his breath back.

Marion kicked the ball at Clyde, "Come on Clyde I will be goal keeper."

The boy never ran out of energy and Clyde stopped the ball, "Okay Marion but I will score so many goals."

"No way," laughed Marion.

The next evening Clyde waited in the field it was getting cold, and he shivered. He kicked the ball between his feet, and rubbed his hands together. The wind was picking up as well, and soon it would be Gail force.

Then a woman came out from around a tree trunk close by, Clyde saw that she wore rags. Her dress fluttered in the wind, and her messy hair went all over the place. She had red hair, and a pale face and bright red lips. She came closer to Clyde and smiled at him, she was very beautiful, and Clyde smiled back at her.

She reached out for him and her eyes turned red, and she opened her mouth to reveal shape fangs.

"Stop no one touches Clyde," Marion cried out, and then he was upon the woman.

He took her round the neck and pulled her away from Clyde. She tried to fight him off, but the small boy was strong.

"You touch one hair on his head, and my father will hear of it," he cursed at her. The woman stopped fighting, and stood back as Marion let her go.

"You know what that will mean," Marion said, and then the woman was gone.

"Who was that, and her eyes and teeth," Clyde said looking worried.

"Come on Clyde let's play ball," Marion said.

"Will you take me up into the sky again please Marion," Clyde said smiling.

"If you can score ten goals I will think about it," Laughed Marion.

The next evening Clyde did not have to wait long, and Marion was soon besides him.

"How do you do that," Clyde said in wonder.

"Do what," Marion said innocently.

"Move so quick," Clyde replied.

Marion shrugged his shoulders, "It's just something I can do."

"Hey I told my parents about you," Clyde said smiling.

"Good," Marion replied.

"Will you come and eat with us tonight," Clyde said almost pissing his pants in excitement.

"Of course, but will you come and live with me Clyde."

Clyde was a small boy and to him everything was cool, "Yes I will."

Clyde sat next to Marion at the table with his father at the head, and his mother the other side. His father was a small man with a bald head and glasses, his mother was also small and slim with curly blonde hair.

"So, Marion where do you live," asked his father eating a mouthful of greens.

"Do you live with your parents," asked his mother sipping at her glass of water.

"I live with my father a great man of legend," Marion said proudly.

"Really," smiled his father, "Sounds like a great man."

"We would like to meet him some day," added his mother.

"Oh, you will meet him real soon," Marion said and smiled at them.

Then all hell broke loose as the dining room window burst inwards. The figure was quick, and Clyde barely saw what happened.

He sat there as Marion and the tall dark figure drank the blood from his parent's bodies. Then the tall man stood up, and looked down at Clyde he had a bald head and a skeleton face, the bones almost sticking out of his skin.

He had small dark evil eyes and a long nose, "Take him back," the man ordered, and then he was gone.

"Sorry my friend," Marion shrugged, and picked up Clyde.

Clyde was sobbing inside the coffin his friend Marion laid beside him. They had taken him back to a large mansion in the hills.

The man in black had then bitten Clyde, and Clyde had woken up to a new world. He sobbed for his parents he knew they were dead.

But he was starting to feel no pity, and he could feel his body changing. He liked what he felt, and stopped his sobbing.

Marion put his arms round him and hugged him tight and said, "My brother."

The end

C Robert Paul Bennett 2016

9

Don't play with little girls

The man sat in his van watching the super market it was late, and the place was packed with shoppers. He smoked a cigarette, and watched.

He was a thin bean like man with a mane of shaggy brown hair, and a large beak like nose. Frank was waiting for a change to pounce like the predator he was. He lived alone in his parents' house which had been left to him when they died. He was fifty-five and never had a girlfriend, no he liked them young. He had been in and out of jail all this life for abusing youngsters.

Then he saw the little girl, and his heart missed a beat, she was gorgeous. She had blonde curly hair and blue eyes, and a pale beautiful face. She wore a green flowing dress, and was standing alone.

Frank drove the white van right up to the little girl, and jumped out of the cab. Without a word he bundled her into the back. No one seemed to notice, and he quickly got back into the cab, and drove off at speed.

He wanted a good look at her, and pulled over at a lay by. The countryside was dark, and the only sounds were of animals. He took his flash light, and opened the back she was sitting against the wall.

"You move or make a noise and I will hurt you," he hissed at her.

He shone the light in her face, and then over her body she was beautiful alright, and he was getting aroused.

"Okay mister," she said in a sweet voice.

She was a weird one he thought she did not seem bothered at all.

"Just you stay quiet," he hissed at her.

"My lips are sealed," she said, and drew a line a long her lips.

She was certainly weird, and he closed the door time to get her home.

The house was a rundown farm house, and the man bundled her out of the back. He put her over his shoulder, and went into the dark house. He opened a door and turned on the light, and put the girl on the floor.

"Now you behave and I won't hurt you too badly okay," he said giving her an evil look.

"Okay no problem," she replied, and he closed the door.

The room was bare apart from two chairs, and a dirty mattress on the floor, and an open fire place. Frank sighed with relief she was his now, and he was going to have so much fun with her.

He cooked his dinner first, and ate his fish and chips at the table there was a sofa and television at his back. But the farm house was cold and dim, but that is the way he liked it. He rubbed his hands together, and left the dirty plate in the sink. Now to go and have me some fun he thought.

He opened the door, and stood there looking confused there was a fire roaring in the fire place.

"How did you do that little girl," he said in amazement.

Then he saw that one of the chairs was missing how could she have broken up a chair with her bare hands.

"How," he said, and scratched his head.

Then the girl came over to him, and held his hand in hers.

The abuse ran backwards, and he was in some kind of trance he saw his first victim, and then his second. The abuse he dealt out, and then he was in jail. He was talking to doctors, and then taking medicine, then he was out again, and abusing children, then he was back in prison.

The trance went on and on until his last victim before this little girl.

The girl dropped his hand, and Frank came back to reality.

"You are a bad man," said the little girl.

"You are a very bad man," she said again.

It felt like the little girl had looked into his very soul, and suddenly Frank was scared of her, very scared. This was not a little girl at all, but some kind of demon!

He backed out of the room, and closed and locked the door.

Well, he would deal with her now all his lust had gone away.

He picked up a hammer he was going to bash her brains in. He smiled the little girl was too strange by far. He opened the door, and moved into the bare room the fire was still roaring in the fire place.

The second chair was now gone.

He gripped the hammer in his hand, and stopped and looked at the little girl. She was standing by the fire place with her back to him.

"Why did you do all those things to those poor children mister," she said in her sweet voice.

"That is no concern of yours little girl," he said and gripped the hammer harder.

"You are so bad mister, and now I must make you pay," she said still with her back to him.

The man laughed, "Oh really."

She turned round, and he saw the blood shot eyes and the large fangs inside her mouth and she hissed at him, "Yes really."

He screamed as she flew at him, and he dropped the hammer.

Frank woke up and found that his hands and legs were tied tightly, and he was lying on the dirty mattress on the floor. He watched as the little girl ripped a dining table chair apart with her bare hands, and threw the wood into the fire.

"Just to keep you warm mister," she said and smiled at him.

"What do you want of me," the man sobbed his wrist hurt from the plastic ties.

The little girl came close to his face, and breathed her foul breath on him, and he gagged.

"Child abuser I will suck out your blood really slowly," she ran her hand over his face, and smiled her sweet smile.

"I will drain you every day it could take weeks or months or even years before you die," she kissed him on the cheek, and put a gag into his mouth.

The end

C Robert Paul Bennett 2016

10

From the sky

Mark watched the sky as he used to every night he was back home with his parents and sister in a farm house. He was twenty-one with short dark hair, and a goatee beard that he thought made him look hard. But the truth was it made him look like a teenager trying to look like a man.

He was still at collage training to be a vet, but he was on his holidays now. Back in his old bedroom, and back to looking at the sky just like he did when he was young. Then Mark saw the comet shooting across the sky it landed in his father's field.

"Holy cow," he said silently to himself.

He could hear the television on, and sneaked out of the back door.

He only had his trainers on, and he cursed as the wet got inside, it had been raining all day. He walked through a field and over a fence not far now. He saw the green glowing by a group of trees it seemed to radiate right through them. He walked up to the green glow cautiously. He walked into the trees, and saw the large hole in the field it was the size of a van.

In the centre of the hole was a pod like thing which glowed green. He went into the hole, and up to the green pod. Suddenly the pod split open, and green goo spat out, and covered Marks face. He spat and coughed, but he had swallowed some of the stuff. Then a large blob of green flew out of the pod, and attached itself to Marks face.

Then the blob of green slid down his throat a spike at its back and then it was gone, and Mark fell onto his back.

Cara Mark's sister was getting ready to go out, and she looked at herself in the full mirror. She was wearing transparent bra and panties, and she looked good. She was a slim girl with small firm breasts, and a mound of brown pubic hair. She had long brown hair, and a pretty looking face. She put on her dress and shoes, and headed out. Any man who picked her up tonight would be in for a treat.

She went outside, and over to her father's car he had allowed her to borrow it for the night. She was singing to herself and just opening the car door when she saw Mark her brother.

"Hey Mark what are you doing out at this time," she said she thought he was a bit of a freak.

Mark stopped by the car and did not say a word.

"Cat got your tongue mark," she said, but there was something odd.

She walked over to him and he looked so pale, "Mark are you okay."

Then as she watched he opened his mouth wide and a spike came out of his mouth, and pierced her shoulder. She cried out, and then she saw her blood being sucked up through the spike, and into Marks mouth. It worked quickly, and soon Cara was drained, and just an empty shell.

Mark dragged the body over to some trees, and left it there.

The body was found the next day by a man walking his dog.

Mark was in the basement listening to the police upstairs, his parents were crying. He smiled he was no longer Mark. But the light hurt him badly, and he had to stay out of the light. The being inside him needed blood to survive. The being was just a soldier being sent ahead to see if they could survive on human blood. He could not wait to tell his superiors that they could.

But they would have to do something about the sun light, the being was sure they could come up with something. The police were looking for him they had already been down in the basement. They would never find him years ago he had knocked out some of the wall, and made a secret hiding place.

It was a place he used to go when he was pissed off with the world.

The being knew everything about Mark.

Donavan sighed and looked at the second drained body, it was just awful. He had been working in the small village as the police captain for two years, and had never seen anything like it. A body drained of all its blood looked like a bag of bones, just skin and bones it made him shiver.

He was a tall man, and plump with a big beer belly he had dark hair, and a moustache. The body sack as he thought it had green goo on it, same as the first body. He had sent it away to the lab, but so far nothing. He had to get to the bottom of this before more bodies started to turn up. But what was he dealing with a vampire.

He looked over the fields, and looked at the farm house in the distance. The farm of the dead girl.

Terry and Russell were out hunting, and the two men moved silently through the woods. Terry was thirty-two, and he was a big man with a beard, and brown messy hair. He was large like a bear and wore a thick hunting jacket and trousers.

Russell was a small man who was clean shaven, and had dark long hair tied back in a pony tail. They saw a deer and Terry put his hand on Russell's shoulder and pointed Russell nodded his head, and the men split up.

Russell went into some trees, and stopped there was a large crater in the ground. He looked and saw pods that had been opened the shells had green goo on them. Then he saw spiky plants surrounding the hole, plants that he had never seen before.

"What the fuck," he said out loud he forgot about the deer.

Terry came into the trees his face red with rage, "What the fuck did you do that for the deer has legged it now."

"Sorry mate but look at this," Russell pointed to the spiky plants.

They stood in the dirt, and were oval with spikes all over, and green in colour.

"I never seen plants like that before," Terry said and then added, "Come on let's take a closer look at them."

Russell shrugged they looked harmless enough, "Okay mate."

The two men bent down, and looked at the plants it happened quickly. The two men were spiked by the plants, and they lay on the ground panting. Then the spike plants opened to reveal a green mass within, a spike at one end.

The green goo slid across the ground, and went into the men's mouths.

The being inside Mark needed blood badly, and Mark ran through the woods, and came into the village. He slowed down, and walked down the quiet streets under the street lights. Then he saw a tramp in an alley way. The tramp was drunk, and did not even see Mark towering over him. Mark got on his knees, and a long spike came out of his mouth, and pierced the tramp.

He sucked up the tramp's blood, and soon the tramp was an empty shell. It was not enough the being needed more blood, and Mark set off for the town.

He came to a house at the end of the village slightly away from the rest of the houses. A light was on, and the being went up to the front door and knocked. The door was opened by a woman in a night gown.

"Yes, can I help you," she asked her hair done up in hair pins.

Mark opened his mouth, and the spike came out, and spiked the woman in the neck.

"Henry," she managed to cry out.

Henry was a tall thin man, and he saw his wife collapsing to the floor he did not hesitate, and took up his shot gun. He saw the young man on his door step, and fired both barrels into the man's chest.

Mark flew backwards and precious blood splattered out of his torn body. But as he landed green goo came out of the wounds, and they started to heal over. The man holding the shot gun saw the young man healing, and the green goo, and ran for his life.

Mark stood up he still needed more blood.

Mark was too slow, and he was walking the streets when the police car spotted him. He saw the man with the shotgun in the back pointing at him.

Mark ran as fast as he could, but the car was faster he cut into the woods, and the police car stopped. He heard men getting out and shouting. He ran all the way home the men close behind it was almost light now.

He ran into the basement from the outside, and closed the wooden shutters behind him. But the men were on to him, and he stood panting in the basement as they came down.

Donovan had a hand gun and he pointed it at the young man, "The games up Mark," he said in a stern voice.

"Watch you don't get that green shit on you," the man with the shot gun said.

"That stuff healed the gunshot wounds I tell you," Added the man.

"Okay constables hand cuff him, and take him outside," Donovan said to his two constables.

As the men approached Mark a spike came out of his mouth.

"Careful men stand back," shouted Donovan, and picked up a shovel that was leaning on the wall.

The spike came out longer now, and Donovan hit the spike with the shovel the spike severed, and fell to the floor. It wriggled on the dirty floor like a snake green goo coming out of the end.

Green goo came out of Marks mouth, and he spluttered and coughed.

The two constables grabbed him, and dragged him up the stairs careful to avoid the green goo. Donovan looked at the piece of spike on the floor it had turned green, and bubbled as it melted.

"What the fuck is going on," he said to himself then followed his men outside.

As Donovan came out of the farm house, he saw Mark screaming on the ground the two constables had stepped away from him. The other man with the shotgun stood, and watched in dumb struck fear.

As they looked on Mark began to melt in the sun light, and soon he was a puddle of bubbling green goo.

"How the fuck am I going to write this on up," Donovan said in horror.

It had been a hard day, and two more reports of dead drained bodies had come in. They had killed Mark, but there was something still out there killing, and draining its victims. Donovan left the police station, and headed home he was beat.

Richard one of the constables left the police station just after Donovan. This was a nightmare he had joined the village police because he wanted the quiet life. This thing was well out of his league, and it scared him badly. Seeing that man melt in the sun light would haunt him forever.

He sighed and walked up to his car, and paused there was something by the trees watching him.

"Hey who is that," he called out.

Then the dog came into the light of the car park, it was Jessie she often came to the police station for treats. They all spoilt her even if she did come from a good home down the road.

Richard walked up to the dog and got down on his knees and stroked her, "Hello Jessie."

The dog opened its mouth wide, and a spike shot out of its mouth, and imbedded itself into Richard's throat.

The end

C Robert Paul Bennett 2016

11

Blood snake

When the military base went up in smoke everyone in the town below thought 'oh no.' There had been rumours for years about secret experiments going on at the base. If the place had gone up in flames, then what could have gotten out. But all the local papers and army chefs assured the town that nothing had ever been going on up in the base.

Even the army major got in on the act, and went on television to say there had never been any experiments at the base. It was used as a warehouse, and had caught fire, and that was it. There were no animals there, and no one had been injured the major assured the town.

So, the sleepy town at the bottom of the hills went back to its normal life.

Ted laughed at a joke, and looked out over his back garden it was late, and the party was in full swing. They had a barbeque earlier, and now the drink was flowing. The music blared out, and people danced in the garden. It was Ted's sixth birthday, and he was a well-liked person.

He saw some kids playing by his garden pond, "Hey you be careful not to fall in," he said smiling.

The kids waved at him, and carried on playing 'bless them' he thought.

He was a thin man with grey hair and a moustache. He wore white slacks, and a green jumper.

"Lovely party Teddy," said a rather drunk woman kissing him on the cheek. He looked around, but could not see his wife, Alison.

They had been married for thirty years, and she was still the love of his life. Their children had all grown up, and lived aboard so they could not be here tonight. He leaned against the wooden garden fence, and took a sip of his gin and lemonade.

He never knew what hit him.

Something came through the fence, and grabbed him, and then he was gone!

The drunken woman saw the hole in the fence and went over, "Teddy," she said.

The giant snake took the man in its jaws, and injected him with poison the man stopped moving. The snake found a quiet place, and then put its fangs into the man's body and drank. The snake needed blood, and when the man was exhausted the snake left the body on the ground.

Kenny waited and held his breath, but the deer jumped off into the woods. Damn it he had no luck all day, and was getting pissed off now. He loved to hunt on his own at weekends that was how he got away from the rest of the world.

Just him and nature, and then the thrill of the hunt, and the kill.

Kenny was a small man and thin with it, he had messy dark hair and a beard which he kept well trimmed.

He was thirty-five and married with three kids, and this was also a way of getting out of the house at weekends. He would hunt Saturday and Sunday till late taking a packed lunch with him. His wife did not mind, and he had suspicions that she was having an affair.

"Fuck it," he cursed he was not going to get nothing today not even a hare.

He heard the noise close by, and looked to his left he could not see anything. It had sounded like something big coming through the under growth. He took aim, and aimed his rifle at the bushes and trees nothing moved, and it seemed to have gone deadly quiet. Then the bushes parted, and he saw the biggest snake he had ever seen.

The snake reared up and its evil eyes looked at him, and then the snake took Kenny in its mouth, and injected him with poison. Kenny dropped the rifle, and stopped moving the snake moved off holding the man in its jaws. It stopped a little way out, and then put its fangs into the man's body, and drained him dry. It left the body on the ground, and slithered off.

Jack and Vera loved coming here for their holidays, the wooden cabins in the countryside away from everything. There were seven cabins in a group, and they came here every year.

Jack and Vera were both retired, Jack had owned his own pub for many years, and Vera had worked with him. Now they both enjoyed life, and taking it easy. Their children were all grown up, and living their own life's.

Jack had curly brown hair and sat down, and rubbed his big belly, "That was lovely my dear," he had just finished his ham sandwich.

"Glad you enjoyed," Vera replied she was also a big woman with large breasts and hips.

She ran a hand through her grey hair, and looked out the window in the kitchen. Jack saw her come into the living room from the kitchen, and she was staring with her mouth open.

"What's up love you look like you've seen a ghost," he said getting up from the chair.

The side of the cabin exploded in a shower of wood, and Jack hit the floor hard. Pain went through his shoulder, and he saw the creatures head inside the cabin. The giant snake took the woman in its jaws, and was gone Jack got to his feet and held his shoulder.

He walked to the smashed wall, and screamed as the snake came back and took him also. He went quiet as the poison entered his body.

The snake would feed well on the two humans.

"Did you fucking see that," Hector cried out grabbing his mobile phone.

He was a large man with short dark hair, and a rough unshaven look about him. He also had a large belly that wobbled in front of him.

"No what darling," said his wife, Juanita.

His chubby face had gone white, and he called the police.

"A giant snake I swear on my children's lives," he said to his wife pointing outside.

Juanita looked and saw one of the cabins had a massive hole in its side. She put her hand over her mouth and said, "Oh my god."

The police cordoned off the cabins, and the other two occupants were put into a hotel for the night.

The army sent up helicopters, and searched the area. They knew what they were looking for. Captain Johnson smiled without humour. The damned snakes had escaped in the blast at the army base. He was a tall man and lean and muscular he was forty, and bald with hard mean eyes.

A male and a female god knew what would happen if they had mated.

The helicopter was loaded with a missile that would take out the snakes. The snakes were big, and would be easy to find he hoped. His career was on the line if the public found out about the snakes his arse was history. The project was his baby, and the snakes were going to be used in a war situation.

The project was in its early stages when the blast had hit the army base, and the damned monsters had gotten out.

"We got one sir," said the pilot.

"Then blow the fucker to hell," shouted Johnson.

Johnson watched, and then he saw the snake below it was moving quickly, and heading for the river.

"It must be living in the river or a cave off the river," shouted Johnson.

The helicopter followed, and then there was a blast as it sent out the missal. The shot was good, and the snake exploded as it reached the water.

A shower of blood went up into the air.

"Good now let's get the other one," Johnson shouted.

"Okay sir we will hunt down river," said the pilot.

The giant snake watched as the helicopter went over head, the beast was lying in a cool cave. It had heard the blast, and could smell death in the air, the death of its partner. The large snake moved deeper into the cave. It was cool inside the cave, and the snake rested its body it would soon need blood.

A short distance away from the cave on the river bank there was a hole. Inside the hole were ten eggs which the female had laid earlier, the male snake had fertilized them. The eggs were left in a warm place to hatch. The speed of the giant eggs was quick, and the eggs were due to hatch at any minute.

The end

C Robert Paul Bennett 2016

12

Infest

The old woman stood outside her back door, "Royce come here boy," she called to her dog. She lived in small cottage in rolling fields, one field had been sectioned off, and that was her back garden.

The woman had curly grey hair and a wrinkled up old face, she was small and large with wide hips.

"Come on Royce I have a treat for you," she called again.

Then she heard the dog whining in the long grass, and she hurried inside to call the vet.

Ricky was a tall skinny man with light brown hair, and a silly looking moustache. It was like a brown slug on his upper lip. He was forty, and still fit he worked out at the local gym he was single, and had been for a while, and he kind of liked it that way. Ricky marched into the back garden Jean was always calling him worried about her dog Royce. He smiled the old woman kept him in a job.

He hunted through the long grass, and stopped dead the dog was on the ground its tongue hanging out of its mouth. Its body looked deflated as if something had sucked the dog dry, and the dog had red marks all over its body.

Ricky put the dog's body in a zip up body bag this would have to go to the lab. He scratched his arm, and saw red marks on his skin. He hurried out of the back garden, and told the woman her dog had died of old age, no point in upsetting her.

A few days later and Ricky still had those red marks on his skin, but they did not scratch anymore, and they were fading slowly. Something had bitten him in that back garden maybe the same thing that had killed the dog.

The lab results were on his desk that morning, and he opened the envelope. He read the report and his eyes went wide, "Flea's," he said out loud.

The report said that the dog had died of thousands of flea bites the fleas had sucked the blood out of the dog's body. A new strain of flea's the report said.

Ricky got on the phone he had to call the environmental agency.

John was a short man with brown hair and glasses, and he wore a blue suit and tie. Not the best thing to wear for outside work thought Ricky. They parked by the old woman's cottage, and walked up to the front door, the door was open.

"Jean you there," called Ricky, but there was no answer.

"Maybe she is out," John said shrugging his shoulders.

"No, she wouldn't leave the door open," Ricky said and walked into the cottage.

They found Jean on her bed dead, red marks all over her body.

John and Ricky started scratching, and fled the cottage.

In the car John said, "I read the lab report about these damn fleas we got to burn this land."

Ricky nodded his head and scratched at his legs, "Damn right."

Ricky stood and watched as the army personnel burned down the cottage, and burned the fields around the cottage. The smoke rose into the sky, and the smell of burning was powerful on the nose.

Jeans body had been taken away earlier. Ricky smiled at least they would get these damn fleas he still had red marks on his arms and legs.

In a couple of hours, it was all done, and Ricky got in his car and drove home.

Ricky only lived half a mile away from Jeans cottage in the town.

He sat down after making his dinner, and turned on the television. He watched a documentary on shame marriages, and thought why bother.

But people were desperate to get into England, he did not feel sorry for any of them, they were breaking the law at the end of the day. Then he watched the news, and leaned over and picked up the remote, and turned the sound up. Reports were coming in from all over the country of bites. The news showed a man's red arm the marks were the same as Ricky's.

"Oh my god," Ricky said.

The news even reported two deaths which details were not being released at this time. There is no cause for panic said the reported looking smugly into the camera.

Ricky sighed, and turned the channel over this was bad news. He sat there, and wondered what he could do. He would phone John in the morning, and arrange some kind of meeting. They would have to canvas the town, and see if anyone had bite marks.

He heard a scratching at the back dog, his dog Lucy was out.

He got up from his chair, and walked over to the back door and let her in.

"Hey Lucy girl," he said smiling at his dog a greyhound.

Then he saw the red marks on her body, and ran his hand down her fur.

"Damn it," he cursed rubbing his hand something had bitten him.

The end

C Robert Paul Bennett 2016

13

Members only

The office was quiet save for the usual printer noise, and the coughing of someone at their desk. The rain poured down outside, and London looked a bleak place. Adam sat at his desk he was twenty-four, and had worked for the tax office for six years since leaving school.

He was a short man with brown curly hair, and a cheeky smile. He sat next to his friend Louis who was the same age, but had only been at the tax office for four months. He had short blonde hair, and blue eyes set in a handsome face.

It was Adam who had gotten him the job.

"Hey Louis I heard last night about a special club called members only," Adam sat looking at his handsome mate.

"Really what's so special about it," Louis replied not really interested.

"They say it's like the masons you have pilots, surgeons, doctors even MPS," Adam paused.

He saw that Louis was not interested, but finished anyway, "So if you get in trouble, you can call in favours that's what I heard."

"Sounds very interesting, and who told you that anyway," Louis said now looking at his mate.

"Jason last night said he found it on the net," Adam said.

"Jason is full of shit," Louis laughed.

Adam just shrugged.

But Louis was interested, and that evening he surfed the net looking for this special club. He was surprised that he found it so quickly, and indeed it was there on his screen members only. He looked at the site there was not much only an e-mail address to post your application.

'Please send a written letter saying why you want to join, and two recent pictures of yourself. There is no guarantee of being accepted you must be special.'

That was it and the e-mail address, Louis wrote down the e-mail address might as well give it a try he thought.

Louis attached two recent pictures of himself to his e-mail, and thought he looked very handsome even if he did say so himself.

He wrote after dear sir/madam.

I am Louis and I am twenty-four as you can see from my pictures, I am a good-looking guy, and sometimes do modelling.

I am very keen to join your special club, but wonder why it is so special. I am single now and my hobbies are watching horror movies, and I write short stories.

I have heard that your club has well respected members, and I can offer something back to them.

He left his name at the bottom, and sent the e-mail. Short and sweet let us see what happens.

The bit about modelling was bullshit, but what the hell they were not to know that.

The next day at work Louis sat at his desk working on his computer. Adam was seated at the next desk, and he turned to Louis.

"Jason tried to get into that members only club they said no," Adam said and laughed.

"That's because Jason is an ugly bastard," Louis replied smiling.

Louis checked his e-mails, and saw one from the members only. His heart was racing as he opened the e-mail.

Dear Louis

Thank you for your application at this time I can reveal no details about our members only.

If you wish to continue meet our man at the train station on Saturday at ten in the morning. He will know who you are.

Also please do not tell anyone about this letter or the meeting will be called off.

The decision is yours Louis.

It was signed members only at the bottom.

"Anything interesting," Adam said trying to see over Louis shoulder.

Louis logged out of his e-mails, "Nope just the usual spam."

Louis arrived at the local train station, and got a coffee from the booth. He looked up and down the station people were reading papers or doing stuff on their mobile phones.

He waited for half an hour, and was going to give up when a tap on his shoulder made him turn round. He looked down at a small man with a bald head and glasses.

"Louis I am Butler pleased to meet you," the man held out his hand, and Louis took it.

"You are from members only," Louis said excitedly.

"Yes, my friend now let's catch the next train," said the small man.

They rode in silence most of the way, "So tell me about the club Butler."

Butler smiled at him and shook his bald head, "Sorry Louis."

They arrived at Tottenham court road, and the shopping crowds were already starting. He followed Butler through some back streets, and was wondering where the hell they were going.

Now the back alley looked like a slum, surely the club could not be down here.

"Butler, are we nearly there," Louis said getting pissed off now.

Butler stopped and walked up to Louis, "Yes Louis we are here."

Louis looked around at the old buildings most of them were falling apart. Then he felt a prick in his leg, and looked down and rubbed his leg. He thought he saw a needle in Butler's hand.

Then he started to feel faint, "Butler I don't feel so good," he managed to say.

But Butler was smiling, and holding him up.

Louis woke up later, and shook his head he had the weirdest feeling. He looked around the room he was hanging upside down.

His hands were tied behind his back.

He looked up and saw that his feet were tied to a metal pole that went across the room. He looked round the large elegant room it was full of portraits and tapestries. It looked like some kind of old ball room you saw in the old black and white movies. Rich men and women dancing as the old music played.

The room was empty, but there was a table close to him filled with wine glasses. They looked like crystal and expensive.

Everything about the room shouted out money.

He felt a pain in his neck and tried to see what was coming out of his neck. He looked down, and saw the plastic tube with a tap at the end. He had a plastic tube in his neck with a tap on why the hell was that. He could see the transparent tube filled with his blood.

Then a door opened and a line of people wearing masks came into the room. They were talking and laughing as they lined up in front of the table with the wine glasses on.

"Damn he looks like a fine fellow," said one man wearing a deer mask.

He picked up a wine glass, and opened the tap on the end of the tube.

Louis saw his blood fill the glass, and then the man turned off the tap and took a sip. He held up the glass to the others and proclaimed, "Damned good vintage enjoy my friends."

Another man stepped up and took a wine glass, and filled it with Louis blood. He took a long sip and sighed and said to the waiting crowd, "Damn fine taste full bodied, and it appeals to my palate."

There were murmurs of satisfactions from the crowd, and they looked at Louis hungrily.

The end

C Robert Paul Bennett 2016

14

The sucking pit

1960's

It was the end of the nineteen sixties, and the war raged on in Vietnam.

Keith checked his machine gun it had been a bloody hard war so far, and the Americans were no closer to winning. He had seen many of his men die, and had loads of blood on his own hands.

Keith Jackson was a tall well-built man with short dark hair and a beard. He had rugged weather-beaten features. The Vietnamese were forcing them back, and his troupes followed him.

Damn this war he thought. The heat was over powering even in the night. The jungle was full of insects, and wild animals. Keith and his six men were forced back into a group of trees.

"We stay there for cover," he shouted a bomb exploded close by.

Gunshots and screaming men could be heard in the distance. Then an army of Vietnamese men were close by and Keith thought this was it, but they stopped and started to jabber.

"What are they saying," Keith asked Bruce a young man who could speak the language.

"They are saying we are in the sucking pit," Bruce said his face dirty with mud.

The ground was soft and some of the men started to cry out.

"The sucking pit will suck the life out of us, we are dead," Bruce said.

Keith felt himself sinking in the mud, and soon he was the only one left his head poking out of the mud, "Please god have mercy on my soul, and look after my family."

Then he was gone, and the dirty brown mud changed to red.

1980's

Martin Jackson was on his way to Vietnam, and he wondered what he would find. He was the younger brother of Keith who had died in the Vietnam War.

But he had found a new lead that suggested that Keith may have been killed by nature instead of man. His body, and that of all his troupes had never been found. Martin had come across the sucking pit on line, and had read with interest. He kept all his notes in the attic back at home.

Home where his wife Lisa and boy Toby were, and he would miss them both. Martin was tall like his brother, but he was skinny with blonde hair and a goatee beard. He had made friends on line with a man who claimed to know all about the sucking pit.

The man would meet him at the airport.

At the airport the man was small with a bald head, and said his name was Lee Keung.

"Mister Jackson," Lee said in perfect English.

Martin took the offered hand, "Please call me Martin Lee."

After checking into a hotel Martin and Lee went out into the jungle in Lee's van. They drove for an hour, and finally reached a group of trees Lee stopped the beaten-up old van, and climbed out.

"Now we must be careful," Lee said pointing to the trees.

"Is this the place," Martin said it did not look like anything.

"Inside that group of trees is the sucking pit, that is where your brother died, I am sure of that," Lee said.

"But how sure can you be Lee."

"Legend has it that the sucking pit has been here before time its self, and claimed thousands of lives.

There were no bodies found of your brother or his troupe no they were killed in the sucking pit."

"Wow that is some story can we have a look," Martin asked the small man.

Lee took Martin to the edge of the trees, and they peered inside. The trees formed a circle around the soft looking mud the sucking pit.

That evening Martin wrote a letter back home and posted it. He then went out, and got drunk. A sleazy looking man at a bar started talking to him, and offered to take the American to the sucking pit. Martin was telling the man he wanted to go back that he did not believe in the sucking pit.

It was a massive cover up by the government, and his brother was in hiding somewhere. Martin kept on about his theories in the car, and the sleazy man drove.

They reached the trees and the man took all of Martins money, and left him there. Martin rock and rolled on his feet holding a bottle of Jack Daniels.

Not sure what had just happened, "Hey you wanker," he shouted, but the man had gone.

Martin was left alone in the jungle at night he staggered over to the trees.

"Sucking pit my arse," he said out loud and took a long swig from the bottle.

He stepped into the trees, and stood in the circle of mud and began to sink. The dirty brown colour changed to red.

2000's

The airport was packed as the man made his way out holding a piece of paper with an address on it. He saw a spare taxi and got inside and gave the man the piece of paper, "I what to go here," he asked the driver.

"No problem, sir," said the driver, and smiled at him he spoke very good English.

Toby sat back in the seat, and sighed it had been a long old journey.

He carried a suit case, and a big bag that was zipped up. Toby was searching for the sucking pit he was the son of Martin. He had found his father's notes in the attic, and the letter he sent home. The letter had stated that he was staying for a few more nights, and then he would be back. He wanted to visit the sucking pit one more time.

But his father had disappeared, and after all these years he was still missing.

He had read the story of the sucking pit, had it taken his uncle Keith, and his father he was sure that it had. He came to the address and paid the taxi driver, and walked up the drive, and knocked on the front door.

A young girl answered she was real pretty with a pale face and long dark hair, "Can I help you sir," she asked.

"Can I see Lee Keung please," he said and smiled at her.

"Hold on for a minute sir," she replied, and then she was gone.

A small man with a bald head and glasses came to the door his face was wrinkled and old.

"I am Toby, Martin Jackson's son."

They rode in silence through the jungle to the group of trees, "This is the sucking pit," Lee said.

"I showed your father Toby only once, I did not know if he came back as you say," Lee said sadly.

"Thank Lee," Toby put his hand on the man's shoulder and smiled.

"Be careful the soft mud is just inside the trees, I will stay in the car and wait for you," Lee said.

Toby got out of the car, and carried the bag with him to the trees. He peered inside the trees, and saw the circular piece of mud in the middle. He unzipped the bag and took out two reefs one had Uncle Keith the other Martin my dear father.

"Rest in peace Uncle Keith," he said and threw in the reef, and then he said, "Rest in peace dear father."

He watched as the two reefs began to sink into the mud. He turned away from the sucking pit, and walked back to the waiting car.

The end

C Robert Paul Bennett 2016

15

The bloody rose

Room number seven in the hospice was being cleaned out for the next patient. Nurse Williams tidied up the room there was not much too tidy.

A bed one bedside cabinet, and a television hanging from one white wall. A young nurse was helping her.

"Where did you get that rose it's so beautiful," the young nurse asked.

She was slim with long dark hair and a pale white face. Nurse Williams was the opposite she was a heavy-set black woman with neat curly hair.

"Why I got that in a place called Allen town in the countryside," she answered.

"Well, I think it's lovely," said the young nurse.

"Yes, a large mansion looks over the town a lovely place," Williams added.

The rose looked good on the window sill, and its bright red was a contrast to the plain white walls.

Nurse Williams was on her way to see the new patient in room seven he was an old man dying of cancer by the name of

Sidney. She walked into the room, and stopped the old man was sitting on his bed, holding the rose pot in his hands.

"Sidney what are you doing out of bed," nurse Williams asked him.

He looked at her with his tired old eyes and wrinkled face, "The rose needs me."

"Don't be silly now," Nurse Williams said, and put the rose back on the window sill, and the man into bed.

Nurse Williams was sad, but she was used to this as they wheeled Sidney out of room seven. She would change the bed, and get the room ready for the next patient as always. She saw the rose on the bed side cabinet, and moved it back to the window sill.

The rose was a blood red colour, and almost seemed to be shining with life.

Nurse Williams stood at the foot of the bed in room seven as the doctor looked at Hilary in the bed. She was old and she did not have much time left, and her family were waiting outside to see her.

Nurse Williams noticed the rose on the window sill it was a dull brown colour, and leaning over to one side. She would have to throw that old rose out when she next cleaned the room.

The next day Hilary died, and Nurse Williams was changing the bed, and cleaning up the room. She had forgotten about the old dead rose, and put her hands on her large hips when she had finished. She was about to leave when she noticed the rose on the window sill.

It was a bright blood red colour, and it seemed to be shining with life.

"Well, I never," she said going over to the rose.

"Looks like you have made a comeback."

"I put that there," it was the young nurse with the pale face and long hair.

"What do you mean Martha," that was the nurse's name. Williams got on well with her, and they often had tea together.

"Well, it was on the bed side cabinet when they took Hilary away so I moved it back to the window sill."

"I see," Nurse Williams replied.

Room seven had a dying man he was young and handsome he was dying of aids. Nurse Williams would talk to the young man Anthony. She noticed that the rose was dull and brown again before she left her shift.

The next day she spoke to Anthony, "So how are you today, Anthony."

It was a damn shame the young man was tall and dark haired, and handsome, but it had been men he liked.

"I'm not so good had bad dream," he replied trying to sit up in bed. Nurse Williams helped him, "Thank you Nurse."

"Tell me about the dream."

"It was weird I got out of bed, and held the rose in my hand, and then blood flowed out of my hands, loads of it and I slipped in it, and fell down. Then a man in dark clothes came down to me and kissed me on the neck, and then I woke up."

"Very strange, but nothing for you to worry about," Nurse Williams assured him, and patted his hand.

Then she turned to go, and saw the rose it was a brilliant red and shining. How could this be the rose was looking dead yesterday, it was the work of the devil. Nurse Williams picked up the rose, and walked out of room seven.

She threw the rose into a trash bin on the walk home.

Barmy was his name, and he was Barmy by nature he lived on the streets, and knew most of the folk in town. He was known as harmless barmy the likeable tramp. He stopped by the trash bin he had not looked inside this one for a few days. He was a small man, and had a face like a ferret with a long beak like nose, and whiskers on his chin.

He had once had money when his parents had died, and he had been working. But the money dried up, and he left his job. Soon he found himself to be down and out at first it was hard after being used to comforts. But he soon got used to the streets, and living outside. He never bothered anyone, and most people never bothered him.

He rooted through the trash bin, and found the rose in its pot. He held the rose up to the moon light the rose was bright red, and seemed to be shining.

"Wow you are a beauty," he said, and walked away with the rose in his hands.

If he had looked deeper into the trash bin, he would have seen the dead cat at the bottom.

The end

C Robert Paul Bennett 2016

16

The vampire report

The mansion was cold and quiet, and the man sat in a large arm chair. He was wearing all black, and was turning the pages of a popular gossip magazine. He was looking at the story about a couple of real vampires who lived in the city. The man read the article turning the pages with his long slender hands and long nails, and laughed out loud.

A few days later the cold mansion was again ringing with laughter as this time the man had the television on. There was a documentary about the young vampire couple in the city. The man laughed as they told the reporter they had lived for hundreds of years. How they needed blood to survive, and they even showed their fangs, and that made the man laugh even harder.

Now the man was dressed in a smart suit black with a white shirt and red tie. For this game he was calling himself Curt. He had seen, and read enough now, enough was enough these charlatans could not continue to make money out of this. He easily found the flat in the city, and knocked on the door it was opened by a small plump man.

Curt recognized him from the magazine, and the television documentary.

He had brown hair which looked like he had cut it with a bowl on his head. He had green eyes and spots on his face he had not put on any make up to hide those.

"Hello I am Curt I'm a reporter with an American magazine, and I would really like to have your story," Curt said and offered his hand.

"Hi I'm Kevin so you must have heard of us then," Curt took his hand it was warm unlike his own which was ice cold.

Kevin stood there looked at the tall man in the smart suit, "How much will you be willing to pay."

Curt leaned over and whispered a figure into the man's ear, and his eyes lit up, "Of course please come on inside," and Kevin opened the door, and invited him inside.

Curt met the woman Tina she was also plump with large breasts. She had short curly dark which made her look like a lesbian. She was not pretty at all, and had piercings in her ears and nose.

"This is my wife Tina who is also a vampire Curt," Kevin said.

Curt shook her warm hand, "Nice to meet you, Tina."

"Nice to meet you Curt my your hands are so cold," she said.

"It's a cold evening, and I have no gloves," Curt said and smiled at her.

"Curt is doing an article for an American magazine, and he is going to pay," Kevin whispered into Tina's ear, and her eyes went wide.

"You are must welcome Curt," she smiled.

"Can I see your teeth first," Curt said.

Kevin and Tina nodded, and opened their mouths Curt looked closely at the false teeth. They fitted nicely over the real normal teeth. He almost laughed, but kept himself in check.

"Really good," Curt said and took out his note book might as well play the part.

"So how were you made," Curt said sitting down, and pretending to write in his note book.

"I was made over two hundred years ago in the small haven of Oxfordshire my maker was a tall handsome man.

He left me for dead, and I had to make my own way in the world," Kevin said, and Curt yawned.

"Sorry I'm just tired please go on," he smiled at the couple.

"Well, I met Tina about two decades later, and made her like me," Kevin said smiling at his wife.

"Yes, and I'm so glad he did," she said, and took Kevin's hand in hers.

Their stories were too short and boring, but Curt played the part well, and pretended to write.

He sniffed the air, "I'm sure I can smell fish and chips is that what you had for dinner tonight," Curt asked Kevin with a smile.

"I told you we are vampires we only drink blood," Kevin said going red in the face. That was another thing vampires did not blush only after feeding sometimes.

Curt pretended to look closely at his note book, "Now if need to ask you an important question."

Kevin sat up with his wife Tina, and nodded his head yes.

"Have you ever seen or met a real vampire," Curt said and looked at them both.

"Are you seriously asking us that," Kevin said in disbelief.

"Of course I am," Curt smiled.

"Look you will believe in a short while I can assure you," Kevin said getting up.

He was bursting for a piss and a poo, but could not tell that to Curt of course, Curt smiled this was so much bullshit.

"I need to go find something upstairs," Kevin said, and then to Tina, "Make Curt a cup of tea love."

"What do you need to find Kevin the toilet," Curt said he was enjoying this.

Kevin's face went red again, "I have no need for toilets I need to find something important," Kevin was bursting.

He rushed out, and Tina went into the kitchen.

Curt came up behind Tina, and put his hands on her breasts, and rubbed, and felt them up. She smiled, and held his cold hands as he rubbed them. She was a right little hooker thought Curt.

"I like that big boy," she said to him rubbing his crotch and then Curt opened his mouth, and sank his fangs into her white neck.

He drew her blood out quickly, and drained her until she was almost dead. He cut his wrist, and made her drink.

"I will strip you naked you will let all of your bodily waste fluids out," he said to her.

He stripped her, and looked at her large saggy breasts and her shaved pussy. He went back into the living room and sat down, and waited for Kevin to finish in the toilet.

"Did you find what you were looking for Kevin," Curt asked as the small man walked back into the living room.

"No, I couldn't find it at all," Kevin said rubbing his head.

"Never mind at least you had a good shit," Curt said with a wicked smile.

"Look I told you I don't need to use the toilet I am a vampire," Kevin stated.

"You are wrong Kevin," Curt said.

"What do you mean wrong."

"You are not a vampire, but your wife is."

"My wife is."

"Yes, your wife Tina is a real vampire like me." Curt smiled.

"Come in Tina," Curt called to the kitchen.

Tina walked into the living room naked and Kevin gasped, "Get some clothes on."

Curt let his body float to the ceiling until his head touched. He saw Kevin looking at him, and sobbing.

"What is going on," Kevin cried.

Tina came over to her husband and cursed him, "You low life human."

He screamed as his wife took him. Then Tina cut her wrist and made Kevin like her.

Curt lowered himself to the floor once more, and waited for Kevin to come round. Tina took off the man's clothes.

Curt hated these two low lives, but it had been fun turning them into real vampires if only for a short time. The man

Kevin came round, and looked around him with his new vampire eyes.

"My god I feel so strong and hungry," Kevin smiled.

"I feel great my husband," Tina cried out.

"You play with fire, and you get burnt," Curt said to them.

He used his mind, and the two new vampires caught fire and started to run around the room screaming. Curt made his exit, and walked away from the flat he looked back and saw smoke rising into the night sky.

The whole block would go up in flames, and he heard the fire engine sirens getting louder.

The end

C Robert Paul Bennett 2016

17

The oldest game

Larry liked to cruse the streets looking for nice girls, and then he would fuck them for money. But he did not mind at all that is the way he liked it no questions asked just fuck, and thank you mam. He had been paying for sex for the past ten years now, and it was old hat to him. He had fucked all the girls on the street at least once.

He was fat and bald with a piggy red face, and dark small eyes, and a flat nose. Not your Mr. Nice looking at all. He saw the girl and whistled out loud, "Man o man that is gorgeous," he said out loud.

The girl was olive skinned, and wearing a flimsy white dress that barely hid her large breasts. She had long dark hair, and her face was that of a princess. He stopped the car next to her and opened his window, "How much love."

Truth was she was new, and he needed to have her no matter how much she charged. She was even more beautiful close up, and he gulped feeling himself getting hard already.

"I will suck your cock for thirty or you can fuck me for forty," she said in a sweet voice.

"Get in love," he opened the door for her, and she climbed in her dress rode up, and he saw see through white panties.

"Your new round here," he asked as he drove off, he knew a good quiet spot not far away.

"Yes, where are you taking me," she asked.

"I know a quiet place by a field don't worry no one will see us," he said and smiled at her.

"Oh good," she said in a sexy voice, and she touched his hard cock through his trousers, "My who is a big boy," she said.

It felt so good having her hand on his hard cock and he moaned and said, "We are here."

He parked the car up, and turned to her.

An owl perched in a tree looked down at the car as it rocked back and forth, and the screaming noises coming from inside. Then blood splattered on the inside windows, and the owl flew off into the night.

The news reporter Stewart young smiled into the camera, and walked to the scene of the crime. He was standing close to a field.

"This is a spot called lover's lane, and last night there was a brutal murder here."

He was tall with short brown hair, and a clean-shaven face he was smartly dressed, and handsome.

"There are no details at the moment, but we gather the police are baffled by the murder."

He smiled into the camera and there was a shot of the car, and you could see blood stains on the windows.

"The victim has not been named as of yet, but we are expecting that very soon."

Old Jeanie had worked the streets most of her life even now in her fifties she still sold her body. She knew all the girls in this district, and they all stayed on their own territory. She was plump with large breasts, and curly blonde dyed hair she wore far too much make up to try and hide the wrinkles. She saw the beautiful girl on the corner of the street, her street. She marched up to the girl, "Hey you get the fuck of my street."

The girl was even more beautiful close up, and she looked Jeanie up and down and said, "Your Street so you own all of this then."

"Why you dirty whore," Jeanie said her fists clenched.

"Me a whore you can talk you old witch," the girl replied and laughed. Jeanie looked up and down the street there were a few people walking, and she did not want to cause a scene, and get arrested.

"Down that alley way now whore," Jeanie spat at her and marched off.

Jeanie waited in the dark alley, and sighed the girl had gone home, good she thought.

"Hey cunt," the voice said from behind her, and she turned round.

Stewart gave the camera his best smile, he knew he was handsome, and he wanted the audience to know it too.

"The second brutal murder in two days, and both murders are linked to prostitution."

The camera spanned down the alley way, and then showed the chalk out line of the body on the ground.

"At this time police are not saying if the two murders are connected.

As soon as we know we will let you know."

Stewart held the mike to his mouth, and smiled once more, "This is Stewart Young signing off."

Tracy pulled her thin jacket up to her chin the night was chilly. She was only wearing a short mini skirt, and a thin t-shirt and jacket. She had loads of make up on her face, and looked the part. Tracy was a policeman going under cover as a prostitute. They had a serial killer on the loose both bodies had the same strange MO. This was not being released to the public, but both bodies had large amounts of blood drained, and puncture wounds.

Tracy was thirty-five and had short dark hair and green eyes she was pretty, but getting wrinkles. She blamed it on the stress of the job. It was getting so cold now, and she wished she had said no to the assignment. But she was after promotion, and so took the job, but she wished she could have worn more clothes.

She saw the young girl up ahead she was beautiful. What the hell is a girl like that doing selling her body she thought?

She walked up to the girl and smiled at her, "Hi there cold night."

The girl was even more beautiful close up, and she looked Tracy up and down, "I don't fell the cold," the girl said flatly.

"Well, I do its freezing," Tracy said and rubbed her hands together.

"Listen I know where we can get a coffee do you fancy one," the girl asked her.

"That would be grand," Tracy smiled, and followed the girl down an alley way.

She caught up with her, "What about these awful murders that are happening," Tracy asked the girl.

"What murders," the girl replied.

The girl must be living on the moon if she had not heard of the murders, it was head line news around the country.

"Those awful murders two nights in a row, and one was a prostitute," Tracy said trying to jog the girl's memory.

"Oh, those I don't count humans as getting murdered that's feeding to me," the girl stopped.

"What did you just say," Tracy said looking at the girls back.

The girl turned round, and Tracy screamed.

Stewart Young smiled at the camera he was again down an alley way.

The camera showed the chalk out line of the body on the ground, and then showed Steward's face again. He held the mike close to his mouth, "Another murder and this time it was an undercover police woman.

She had been patrolling the streets trying to find the killer which she did in a bad way.

No details are being released, and we do not know the victim's name yet. But we must all be vigil, and especially those women walking the streets."

Stewart smiled into the camera, "Until this man is caught, we must all be careful, Stewart Young signing off."

Dave and Alan had been patrolling the dark streets all night they had the night shift. They listened to U2 on the car stereo, blasting out 'where the streets have no names.' Dave was fifty-two with grey hair, and a hard looking face with a goatee beard.

Alan was tall and thin with brown hair, and a thin sunken face.

"Let's go get something to eat," Alan said he was in the passenger seat.

Dave sighed, "Yeah why not mate."

He started to turn the car around there was a burger place close by.

"Hey look at that," Alan said pointing.

Dave peered through the window screen at the stunning girl on the corner of the street.

"Holy fuck man she is gorgeous," Dave said.

"What the fuck is a girl like that doing selling her body," Alan said.

"Come on let's go and talk with her," Dave said and drove the car over to her.

The girl came over to the police car, "Hello officers," she said in a sexy voice.

"Hi there what are you doing out on the streets," Dave said.

Alan leaned over and added, "There is a curfew on the streets at night now until further notice."

The girl looked shocked, "Oh I didn't know I'm sorry."

"No worries love get in, and we will drive you home," Dave said smiling at her.

"Oh, thank you so much officers," she said and climbed into the back of the patrol car.

The police car sped along a country lane, and then it swerved and crashed into a ditch in the side of the road. An owl watched again as the car bumped from side to side, and the screams came from inside.

The end

C Robert Paul Bennett 2016

18

The dead shift

C.J was in the land of nod when his bed side mobile went off, and he slowly came back into the real world.

"Damn it who the hell is that," he cursed under his breath. He looked at the time six in the morning. He had only gone to bed at one after doing a late shift.

"Yes," he said sharply into his mobile.

It was work, and they wanted him to do the night shift at a morgue. He worked as a security guard, and they said they had been having break-ins.

"No problem I will do it tonight," he said and hang up.

He was sixty and had worked in security all his life, and enjoyed his work. Mind you it took it out of him working the night shifts, but it was more money. He was going grey in patches in his brown hair, and he wore glasses. He had a happy looking wrinkled face. Since his wife had left him ten years ago, he had been happily single.

No children no wife all the money he made was his to do what he liked with. He lay down again, and closed his eyes.

The morgue was a cold place, and he did not like it as soon as he had turned up. It just gave him the creeps imagining all those dead bodies in the drawers. He had to watch the main morgue where the bodies were kept.

He had a chair and a desk that looked over the room there was a metal table in the centre. Then the rows of metal draws along both sides of the room. The room was tiled all over, and this added to the cold feel.

He sat down at the desk, and read a book, there was no site to walk round he could see everything from here. Strange that, but the manager had said that for the past few night's bodies had been stolen.

He shivered, and tried not to think what kind of bodies were behind those draws. Burnt bodies, bodies from car accidents or even murdered bodies. He shivered, and tried to concentrate on his book a western.

The book was good it was about a cold assassin who showed no mercy when he went hunting for villains. But his mind kept wandering the bodies behind the metal draws bothered him big time. He thought he heard noises like the metal draws running on the runners.

He thought about that zombie movie he had watched several nights ago Zombie flesh eaters, and wished he had not. He needed a coffee, and the canteen was just outside the door he got up, and went outside into the corridor, and turned into the canteen. He made his coffee, and came back into the morgue and paused, something was not right.

He put down his coffee, and saw that the sky light was open, and one of the draws was also open.

"Damn it," he cursed.

The next night he took his flask full of coffee his boss had not been too pleased. But saw that C.J needed to drink during the night they had not thought of that. The manager said the body was a flesh one that had just come in that night. He was in a state about the missing bodies, and C.J assured him nothing would happen tonight, he would not leave his post.

After they had made a fool of him last night, he took this personally now, and would find these body snatchers. He had his flask of coffee, and his cheese and ham sandwiches, and biscuits.

He was all set for another night inside the morgue.

He read his western, and kept his eye on the sky light, dare they come through that tonight he thought. He wore a blue uniform, and had a baton on his belt, and he was not scared to use it if he had too. He took a sip of coffee, and ate one of his sandwiches.

It was a horrible night, and the rain lashed down, and made patter, patting noises on the sky light. Then he dropped his book and his heart nearly went into his mouth, he had heard a noise from one of the draws.

"Holy fuck," he panted.

There it was again a banging noise coming from one of the metal draws. It had to be a wind up. He got up and slowly walked along the rows of draws. He paused, and waited, and then it came again, and he found the draw. He gripped the handle, and took a deep breath probably nothing. He pulled the draw open, and it slid along its rails.

He expected to see some kind of animal maybe a trapped bird. He was not prepared for what did come out of the draw.

A man jumped out, and pushed C.J away as C.J went back he saw the man's red eyes, and his long sharp fangs. C.J landed on his arse on the tiled floor the sky light opened, and he saw a man in black up here.

The man in black held out his hand, and the dead person grabbed it, and went up and out of the sky light. The man in black dropped to the tiled floor, he was very tall and wore a hood over his head. But C.J could see his pale face, and red eyes.

The man picked up C.J as if he weighed nothing, and C.J screamed.

C.J woke up and at first, he thought he was back in his flat, and the damned mobile had woken him again. He opened his eyes, and looked around it was in total darkness. He moved, but found he was boxed in the first thought was that he was inside a coffin, and he panicked.

He banged on the walls, and kicked with his feet.

Then he was sliding, and he came into the light of the morgue. The tall man in the hood looked down at him, and held out his hand. C.J took the hand, and the man helped him up, the sky light was open, and C.J was so hungry.

The end

C Robert Paul Bennett 2016

19

Vampire in love

Hi I am Leroy, and I am a black vampire with a love story to tell. Can a vampire fall in love with a human well I did. I will not go into my past too much, but I was a thug and hoodlum in a gang of vicious young men. Lucky for me a meet a vampire one dark night, and was made into what I am now.

I am tall at six three and lean and muscular with short curly hair, and a forever clean-shaven face. This is my love story I write down now. I was hunting one night in this neighbourhood I had never been to.

I was floating in the sky one night, and I heard a voice singing it was like the voice of an angel, and I floated down to an open window. It was a hot night, and I looked into the bathroom of this house, and saw her naked in the shower. She had long blonde hair and blue eyes, and a cute pale white face.

She had firm small breasts, and a dark mound of pubic hair between her legs. Now I do not normally go for white women, but she was special. There was just something about her face, and body that made me fall in love with her right then.

But what could I do I was a vampire and she was a human, I came up with a plan.

The next evening, I waited in the bushes of her front garden, and soon her car drove up her drive way. She had loads of bags of shopping, and I stepped out and asked if I could help her. I sent out a message to her brain, that I was a good man, and could be trusted, but I did not abuse my power too much.

She smiled at me and said, "that would be lovely thank you," and I told her my name. Her name was Annabel, and she invited me inside for a coffee or a tea.

We chatted just small talk, and she smiled at me all the time and I was in heaven. I thought vampires were cold and dead to feelings, but here I was feeling love for this woman. I asked her out on a date, and she said yes to my delight, and I did not use my powers that would have been cheating.

In the Chinese restaurant we talked away the next night, and I put my food into my jacket pockets. I was far too quick for her to see, so she thought I was eating. Then something I could not have fore told happened her ex-boyfriend turned up. He was a rough looking white dude with shaven head, and a goatee beard.

He looked at me and threatened to take me apart so I said OKAY buster outside then. Annabel was crying, and I told her not to worry I would not harm him.

Outside it was over before it started, he tried to punch me, and missed sending him to the ground. He cursed me and got to his feet, and I smacked him on the jaw. He went down hard and he was out for the count. I went inside and got Annabel, and she called him every name under the sun.

But then the real problems started back at her place, I had come back for a coffee, which I would pour into the flower pots. Anyway, we were on the sofa and she started to kiss me, I kissed her back, and her tongue went into my throat. She said something about me being so cold, and how she was going to warm me up.

The thing is vampires cannot make love or anyway I did not have that power. My penis was as dead as a dodo. She started to rub my limp penis through my trousers, and asked if there was anything wrong.

I was in a spot remember, and this had never happened to me before as a vampire. I told her I could finger her and lick her out, but I could not make love. Wrong thing to say like I said this was all new to me, and her face dropped. She was disappointed in me big time I could tell straight away.

She asked me to leave as she was feeling tired so I left her on the sofa.

The next night I came back to her place and rang the door bell. She was nice to me, but said that she did not want to see me anymore. I was upset and walked away feeling rejected, and yes hurt. I walked the streets all night thinking, and I came up with a plan.

I would be her guardian angel, and watch over her always until she died. Any man that tried to hurt her I would punish. So dear reader that is what I am doing now, every night I watch her.

I am happy doing this as eternity is a long time, and she will keep me busy for a good few years.

The end

C Robert Paul Bennett 2016

20

The soul sucker

The little boy laid back in his bed excitedly his blue eyes wide with wonder. The old man sat on the boy's bed, and smiled down at the little boy.

"Tell me the story of the soul sucker granddad," the little boy asked.

The little boy was in his pyjamas, and had short brown hair and a cute little face. The old man was wrinkled of face, and bald of head, he wore trousers and a grey jumper.

The old man laughed, and then cleared his throat.

"Good little boys and girls have no need to worry about the soul sucker," the old man began, and smiled at the little boy.

From outside a dog barked once, and then silence fell once more.

"But if you are a bad little boy or girl then the soul sucker will hunt you down."

The little boy smiled, and gulped at the same time.

The old man moved his butt on the bed and coughed, and then said, "It sucks out your very soul like a vampire would suck out the blood from your veins."

The old man smiled down at the little boy whose eyes were still open in wonder.

"You will find the soul sucker in your wardrobe or under your bed waiting for you to fall asleep.

Then it will creep out and open your mouth, and suck out the souls of bad little boys and girls."

The old man saw that the boy's eye lids were getting heavier.

"So, you be a good little boy now do you hear," the old man said.

The boy nods his little head on the pillow, and closes his eyes and falls asleep. The old man rubs the little boy's hair and kisses him on the cheek, and leaves the room.

The end

C Robert Paul Bennett 2016

21

Eight-legged vampire

Major Glenn Tunney was a happy man his own creation was now complete, and ready for testing. It had been his idea to breed a spider with a growth hormone. The spider had grown big alright, but it was fat and bloated, and useless. But he had come up with another idea why not put the bloated spider body in a metal frame.

The technology now was just too good, and they made a metal spider frame with eight movable legs. An electro was attached to the spider's brain, and it could move the legs as its own. The monster needs blood to survive so a metal spike had been attached to the bloated body. The spike would come out of the spider's metal mouth, and pierce the victim, and then suck up the blood.

The beast was ready for testing when the earth quake happened. The base shook, and walls almost came down. People were running round screaming, and Major Glenn Tunney made his way to the labs. His fear grew as he saw drained bodies along the way.

Then a young army soldier stopped, and shouted at the major, "Get out the monster is loose."

Then the young man was gone, "Damn it all to hell," the major cursed.

Deidre and Elmer owned a small farm just outside of the town they were about a mile away from the town. It was nothing big just a few cattle, and pigs, and chickens. Deirdre was out feeding the chickens she was in her fifties, and had curly grey hair, and a wrinkled-up face. Her pet hate was spiders, and she whistled as she threw out the speed to the chickens.

A dark shadow fell over her, and she turned, and dropped the bowl of seed. She screamed at the giant spider all her fears became reality, and it came for her. She tried to run, but the spider picked her up in its jaws, and then spiked her. It dropped her empty shell to the ground.

Elmer was also in his fifties with a bald head, and a smooth round face. He was making a sandwich when he heard the scream, and looked out the window. What he saw almost made him go insane and laugh his wife was being eaten by a metal giant spider. He got his shotgun, and ran out the farm house, the spider came at him fast, but he managed to shoot both barrels.

He screamed as the spider took him, but green blood ran down the spider's legs.

The spider was injured badly, and it walked slowly along a country lane. It left a green trail of slime behind it as it walked. The army had found the beast, and helicopters circled over head. Major Glenn Tunney was in a jeep close by and was giving out orders. Army soldiers were lining the lane guns at the ready.

The major shouted, "Let the beast have it," the gun fire started and the rows of army men let the spider have it.

The major was secretly pleased the spider worked well, and they would soon have another one made.

But for now, they had to destroy this one he did not want the public to see. The roads had been blocked off for miles, and the spider was trapped. Bullets hit the spider's metal frame, but it had one more trick up its sleeve.

It started to fire balls of cob webs at the soldiers, when the balls hit their target they would open, and wrap up the victims. The spider spiked one soldier wrapped in cob web then another.

"Helicopters now," the major shouted into a radio phone.

Helicopters swooped down, and fired two rockets at the spider. The spider was now on its belly the metal legs were not working anymore, it sat in a pool of green blood. The rockets hit home, and the spider exploded showering the soldiers in green goo.

The end

C Robert Paul Bennett 2016

22

Hell's resort

The two men sat on the edges of their beds drinking whisky and coke. They were on holiday at a ski resort in the mountains of Spain. The room was basic with two single beds a wardrobe, and two bedside cabinets, a small sofa to one side. Draws for clothes, and a small bathroom with toilet and shower.

Peter was of medium height with brown hair, and a thin bird like face. He was twenty-nine and lived for his holidays with Paul. Paul was around the same height with blonde hair, and blue eyes he was the handsome one. He was also twenty-nine, and the two were like brothers.

They did everything together, and were a couple of jokers.

"No condom tricks this holiday Paul," Peter said tasting his whisky.

Two years ago, Paul had used a pen to put a condom up Peters arse while he was in a drunken slumber. Peter thought he had been banged by a bloke, and Paul let it go on for two weeks before he confessed.

"No mate I promise," Paul smiled.

"Right, it's time to hit the town and god help the ladies," Peter said raising his glass.

"Damn right lock up your daughter's the boys are on the town," Paul joined in.

As you can imagine a night out with these two ended in getting drunk, and the ladies were normally safe. They had been in several bars, and enjoyed the evening. They stepped out into the cold, and made sure their ski jackets were zipped up.

"Come on let's go back to the room, and have some whisky," Peter said he felt okay.

"Yes, why not," Paul said he too did not feel too bad.

They saw a beautiful girl sitting on a wall wearing only a short skirt, and a small t-shirt that barely covered her breasts.

"Fuck me slowly look at that," Peter said pointing.

"Man, o man that is nice," Paul replied.

The girl smiled at them she had long dark hair and olive looking skin, and she wore bright red lip stick.

"Hi boys do you fancy a good time," the girl said in a sexy voice.

Paul nudged Peter, "Ask her," Paul said.

"How much for a threesome darling," Peter said.

"You can do anything you want to me for a hundred Euros," the girl replied.

"Fucking hell mate," Paul said nudging Peter again.

In their room both men were in the bathroom, Peter was having a piss, and Paul was making sure he looked good in the mirror.

"You got the money," Paul said to Peter who zipped up his trousers.

"Fuck off you can pay," Peter replied.

"Look fifty each okay after all we are both going to bang her," Paul said and Peter nodded.

"Yes, Paul you look very nice you poof," Peter said laughing.

"Fuck you bird face."

They opened the door, and stepped into the bedroom the girl was naked on the sofa. She had large firm breasts, and erect nipples she opened her legs, and they saw a triangle of dark hair.

"Holy fuck," Peter cried.

Peter got his shirt off and jumped onto the sofa, and started to kiss the girl. Paul was trying to get his trousers off, but hopping on one leg when half drunk, was not a good idea.

He fell over and started to laugh, "Come on mate I'm keeping her warm here," Peter said.

Then Peter turned back to the girl, and saw the long fangs, and the red eyes the girl hissed at him!

"Fucking hell Paul a vampire," he shouted out.

"What do you mean a vampire you idiot," Paul said standing up in his boxers. Then he saw the girl grab Peter, and try to bite his neck.

Paul picked up the bedside cabinet, and smashed it over the girl's head. Peter broke free, and joined Paul standing.

"Fuck me a real-life vampire," Peter said panting.

"Yeah, and she nearly had you mate," Paul nudged Peter.

"Fuck off I would have gotten her off without your help Paul."

"Yeah, sure you would," Paul laughed.

The vampire girl was on her feet, "I am going to drain you both, and then bring you back as my bitches," she hissed at them.

Paul who still had his shirt on was wearing a crucifix, he always wore it.

"I am not anyone's bitch," Paul said, and as she came forwards, he put the cross on her breasts.

She screamed as her flesh sizzled, and then she cursed them, "My brothers and cousins will get you for this," then she was gone like the wind.

"That was intense," Peter said.

"Yeah man I beat a vampire," Paul punched the air.

"Come on hot shot I need a whisky," Peter said getting the bottle from the broken bedside cabinet, which lay on the sofa.

"At least the bottle didn't break," Peter said holding it up.

"Now that would have been bad," Paul said, and laughed.

The two were in bed that morning trying to sleep, but finding it hard.

"Would you have banged her Peter?"

"How could I she was after my blood."

"No say I held her down, and she couldn't get at you then would you have fucked her."

"Yes, I think so mate."

"Imagine that fucking a real vampire."

"Yes, but you would need some cream they are all dried up down there."

"How do you know that Peter," Paul laughed.

"Come on dumbo they are dead it makes sense."

"Yeah, I guess so, but you couldn't get a blow job off them."

"Now try and get some sleep Paul," Peter laughed.

"What if her brothers and cousins do come after us?"

"We kick there arses too."

"Damn right mate."

"Now sleep."

They walked to the bar that night through the thick snow it was a wonderful sight everything being white. The air was so fresh. They passed the same spot as the night before it was empty, and they both looked at each other and smiled.

"Hey you want to fuck with us," a voice called out to them.

It was a small girl, and she was now sitting on that same wall. The wall had been empty seconds ago. She wore a summer dress, and had long dark hair, and a pale cute looking face.

"Vampire," Peter said breathing out cold air.

"Yes, but she is only small fry," Paul said and laughed.

They turned away and then another older voice said, "Do you want to fuck with us."

They turned back to the wall, and now five vampires sat on it looking down at them. The one who spoke wore dark clothes, and a hood over his head. There were two girls wearing t-shirts and shorts, and another man wearing a suit.

"I said do you want to fuck with us humans," hood man said with anger in his voice.

Peter saw the snow mobiles, and nudged Paul, and nodded over to the side.

"Well Mr vampire I don't really want to fuck with you send that horny bitch again, and maybe," Paul said as Peter went for the snow mobiles.

"You burnt my sister," hood man pointed at them.

Paul raced to the snow mobiles as Peter started the engine, he dived on the back, and they set off at speed.

"After them," the vampire shouted.

The vampires were fast and kept up with the snow mobiles, and once the man in the suit came close, and Peter had to bump into him. The man went rolling into the snow, but soon got up again, and gave chase. The snow mobiles were nearly out of petrol, and they were near the sides of the mountains now. The engine coughed and died out, and the machine rolled over the snow and stopped. Paul looked up at the side of the large mountain. The vampires surrounded them, and their red eyes shone in the half light from the moon.

"Now we got you humans," hood man said getting closer.

"What the fuck are we going to do this time," Peter asked.

Paul stepped forwards and said, "I'm not afraid of you."

"What the fuck are you doing Paul?"

"Trust me," Paul winked at his mate.

The vampires stopped, and looked at the human as he was mad.

"Get these clowns," hood man cursed at them.

Paul stood there and raised his arms in the air, and shouted as loud as he could, "I hate fucking vampires."

Then there was a tremor, and then they all looked up as snow slid off the side of the mountain. It came down hard and the vampires tried to take flight, but it buried them all.

Rescue squads were on the scene at first light, and they searched through the fallen snow.

"Hey I can hear something over here," one man shouted to his team.

The team members began to dig in the snow, and suddenly a hand shot out. Like in a cheap zombie movie where a hand comes out of the grave. They dug the man out and a voice said from under him, "Hey I'm here too."

Paul was first out and then he heard his mate, "Leave him be," he laughed.

"Fuck you, Paul."

The two men drank coffee by a snow ambulance they were going to the local hospital in a minute just for a check up.

"How did you come up with that idea big shot," Peter sipped his coffee, and smiled.

"I saw some loose snow, and knew it would not take a lot to dislodge it," Paul said, and smiled at his mate.

"Good job mate." Peter said.

They saw the rescue team stop and come over, "What about the other bodies," Peter asked the man.

"Sorry sirs there are no more bodies."

The end

C Robert Paul Bennett 2016

23

Leonard

Foreword

Leonard had been a tall dark haired handsome vampire, and lived for centuries before he disappeared. It is rumoured he was struck down, and buried by some of the vampires he made. He also liked to dress in old black suits with lacy shirts. He was a fierce cruel vampire, and enjoyed tormenting humans. These are four events in his life found in an old journey author unknown.

1

The war was raging, and the city was in melt down mode. The man was tall and dark and handsome, and he was waiting in the doorway of a building. The rain poured down onto the dim streets, and people hurried to and throw. He was waiting for something, and he smiled as he heard a vehicle coming. His wait had not been in vain he stepped out from the doorway, and made his way into the middle of the road.

The truck came round the corner, but not hurrying, and stopped in front of him. It was a German truck with troops in the back. The driver got out, and held up a hand gun, and told the man to move.

"I have English prisoners in this warehouse," the man replied in perfect German.

The driver seemed to get excited, and soon the troops were out of the back. The driver parked the truck by the side of the road, and followed them into the warehouse.

It was easy for Leonard once the troops were inside his little trap; he was doing this for England he told himself. He looked at each man, and put them into a trance it was so easy, he stripped each man naked, and hang them upside down from hooks in the ceiling. They all looked like sides of beef hanging there. Leonard removed his clothes, and stacked them neatly in a corner.

He then awoke the men from there trance, and smiled as they shouted and screamed to be let down. No one could hear them from inside the warehouse. He then calmly walked down on line on the left, and cut each man's throat with his long sharp nails. Then he walked down the right side, and done the same cutting them deep. He opened his arms, and let the blood spurt all over his naked body. He let the blood splatter into his mouth, and walked down the lines getting drenched in blood.

Soon the blood stopped flowing, and the men were all dead.

He towelled himself down, and dressed in his fine clothes.

"So long since I had a proper bath," he said out loud, and laughed.

2

Leonard hid in the big barn he was in the hay loft, and he could hear everything the young couple said. Brian was twenty-two and tall and handsome with blond hair, and blue eyes. He had a muscular body from the years of helping his father on the farm.

His wife was Tanya she was a small woman, slim with long brown hair, and a plain looking face. Brian's father had died and left him a bit of money now Brian wanted to build up his own farm. It was a start he had the barn and a chicken coop, and two large cows, and two young goats.

He also had a piece of land for growing vegetables, and had spent hours planting seeds. The couple were happy, and looking forward to a nice life together on the new farm.

Leonard smiled from the hay loft he had other ideas for them.

That first night Leonard came out of the barn of course he could have killed all the animals at once, but that would be too easy. No let them suffer a bit. The cows did not like Leonard, and they mooed in protest as he came into their pen.

He feasted on both animals, and left them for dead on the grass they would soon bleed out and die. The couple were in bits the next day they could not afford to lose live stock. All their money had been ploughed into this project.

The next night Leonard went to the vegetable patch, and dug it all up with a shovel. He made sure he dug deep, and over turned all the seeds. He then went into the chicken coop, and killed every single chicken feeding on a few of them. Breaking the necks of the others.

The couple sobbed the next day, and called out the police, the policeman took their statements. They buried all the dead animals, and cleaned up the chicken coop. When the man saw the state of his vegetable patch he almost collapsed.

The final night Leonard fed on, and then killed the two remaining goats. Then he marched to the farm house, and banged on the front door. He could have got in any way he liked, but he wanted to have a bit of fun first. Brian came to the front door, and Leonard pushed him inside.

"Sit down," Leonard commanded.

The man sat and his wife came down stairs, "You sit on the sofa," Leonard said. She looked at her husband, and he nodded she sat on the sofa.

"You two are probably the unluckiest people around these parts I chose you at random," Leonard said, and laughed.

"Why us did you kill all of our animals," Brian asked the man.

"Of course I did," Leonard said to the man, and laughed loud.

"You fiend," Tanya said tears in her eyes.

Leonard went over to Tanya and looked into her eyes, and then he held her and ran his hand over her breasts.

"What the hell," Brian said getting up from his seat.

Leonard looked at him hard and said, "Sit down human."

Leonard bit into the woman's neck, and started to drain her keeping his back to Brian it was pure pleasure.

"Please give me back my wife," Brian sobbed.

Leonard tore off the woman's head, and threw it into Brian's lap, "There she is now stop crying."

Brian gasped and threw the head away, and got to his feet Leonard just laughed at him. He then took the man Brian and drained him now Leonard was filled to bursting. It was like being drunk when you had too much blood, and he liked the feeling.

He walked away, and with his mind he set fire to the farm house.

3

Leonard was bored, and walked the dark streets what could he do to amuse himself. Then he came up with a plan he had seen a murder mystery movie the other night, and got the idea from that.

He chose a house at random, and entered the building they had left an upstairs window open. The house was owned by a Martin and Lisa Lynch. They had no children just the two of them no pets.

He came into the bedroom, and made the man Martin sleep. He took the woman and cut her throat with a knife, and let her bleed out. He then hit Martin over the head with a house phone, and put the phone in her hand. He put the knife in Martins hand then dropped it to the floor. He laid Martin on the floor as if he had been hit. Then he went outside, and phoned the police saying someone was screaming in the Lynches house.

The man Martin was arrest and put into jail the trail lasted for a week, and he was found guilty.

He was put into his own cell away from other prisoners, the case had been high profile, and people wanted him dead. Leonard came to the prison, and floated up to the man's cell. He looked in from the outside window.

"Hey Martin how are you doing mate," Leonard said in a cheery voice.

The man gasped, "How," he said.

His cell was on the top floor of the prison about fifty feet high.

"Oh, don't you worry about how I'm here I just am," Leonard smiled at the man.

"I'm going crazy," Martin said, and put his hands over his head.

"Martin," Leonard shouted the man looked at him.

"You don't know me because you were asleep when we met."

"Asleep," the man replied.

"Yes, I killed your wife, and set you up buddy," Leonard laughed.

The man started to bang the walls screaming, and Leonard laughed louder. After a few more nights of going crazy they transferred Martin to an asylum.

Martin was on a bed in a white room he had a straight jacket on. Leonard easy broke the bars at the window, and entered the room.

Martin looked at him and said, "You," Leonard bowed, "Yes, it is I."

Leonard had grown tired of the game, and was going to end it now. He ripped the straight jacket off, and punched the alarm button and waited.

"This is your chance Martin," Leonard winked at the man.

Two big men came into the room holding batons. They saw the ripped straight jacket on the floor, and then Martin jumped them. He scratched and clawed at them even biting one on the arm, but they soon beat him senseless with the batons.

Then Leonard appeared, "Hello guys," he said and laughed as they looked at him in shock horror.

His eyes were pure red, and his teeth long and sharp. Leonard ripped the men apart. He threw arms and legs around the room, and decorated it with their intestines. He fed and drained Martin putting him out of his misery at last. The room was a glory mess, and it would be the talk of crime labs for years to come.

Leonard made his exit, and floated up into the night sky.

4

Leonard was sleeping under a grave slab he had almost been caught out in the light of day. He had hurried into the old cemetery, and opened the grave slab.

He could hear music above him, and smiled what a piece of luck. Three young men were drinking beer, and cheering as a girl danced on top of the grave slab. She done a real sexy dance swaying her hips and the men began to shout, "Off, off, off."

The girl slipped off her t-shirt and they cheered, and then she stepped out of her skirt. She danced in her panties and bra, and then removed the bra. She had firm small breasts with hard nipples then she slipped off her panties, and the men went wild. She danced there naked showing off her shaved pussy, and firm breasts.

Then Leonard threw of the grave slab, and the girl went flying into the air. The three young men looked in shock horror at the figure coming out of the grave, and ran.

The girl was badly hurt she had hit her head on a grave stone blood ran into the grass of the grave. Leonard left her it would be a miracle if she made it through the night.

One man separated from the rest, and ran blindly into a group of trees he bumped into one, and fell to the ground sobbing. He was a fat man with a red chubby face, and he got back to his feet, and rubbed his head. Leonard was hiding on the other side of the tree and he poked his head round and said, "Boo."

The fat man shit himself he really shits his pants, and sobbed like a baby. Leonard took the fat man, and drained him. He left the body on the floor fuck it they could think what they liked when they found it.

Leonard found the other two hiding in an old crypt, he opened the door and then closed it behind him, "I know you are in here," he said and laughed.

He could see perfectly in the dark, and the two boys hid behind an old wooden coffin. There were a few coffins inside the tomb.

"Please mister we saw nothing," begged a thin boy.

"Yes, we won't tell anyone honest," said a smaller boy.

"Oh, I know you won't," Leonard said to them both.

Leonard lit a candle and said, "I want to show you boys something."

He opened one of the old coffins, and took out a skeleton an arm fell to the ground.

He began to dance with the skeleton and said, "There is still life in the old girl even now."

The two boys were sobbing, and getting on Leonards nerves he dropped the skeleton. He cleaned out two coffins, and made the boys lay in one each. He closed the smelly old coffins, and sealed them with his mind.

He walked to the crypt door and went outside, and sealed the metal door using his mind again. The boys were screaming inside the crypt and banging on the wooden coffins, but they would never get out.

Leonard smiled, and walked away.

The end

C Robert Paul Bennett 2016

24

Modern day Dracula

Letter to Greg Carney right sale estate agents   10th July 2015

Dear Mr Carney

I am an old man living in Romania in the mountains in an old place. I wish to move to Kent England, and I am very interested in the property on your books Loughton house.

Please send one of your representatives to me I will pay his air fares and travel. I do not own a computer or mobile phone so forgive for writing letters only.

Yours sincerely

Count Dracula

Letter to Count Dracula   21st July 2015

Dear Count Dracula

I read your letter with interest, and have had that property on my books for a long time. I would love to be able to sell the old place.

I am sending James Beytagh a good young man who will aid you in everything you need.

Yours sincerely

Greg Carney

<u>Letter to Laura Dillon 23rd July 2015</u>

Dear Laura

I have arrived in Romania, and the castle is like something out of a horror movie. Honestly, I can see bats circling the towers.

The count is not so old, and seems to be able to move around very well. Sorry I have to write letters, but there is no wifi or signal for my mobile. I have shown the count the pictures of Loughton house, and he is very keen to purchase the property.

I know you hate snail mail, and like your e-mails and texts, but please write if you can.

I miss you my darling I will be back in a few days.

PS the mail is quite quick.

I love you

James Beytagh

<u>Diary of James Beytagh 24th July 2015</u>

Last night I decide to wander round the old castle, the wind was howling outside, and the rain started to come down.

I could hear the rain hitting the outside of the castle. As I walked down one corridor, I thought I heard girls giggling. It was very strange indeed, and I could not locate where the noise was coming from so, I gave up. I had the strangest dream as well, and I thought wolves were howling outside my window. But of course there was nothing there, and I went back to bed undisturbed.

Letter to Laura Dillon   25th July 20015

My dearest Laura

You probably have not got my first letter, but I find I must write to you to keep me sane. The Count is an odd fellow he only seems to come out at night.

The days are boring, and I wander around the castle, but a lot of the doors are locked. There is a village close by, and I took a taxi there, and had a look round. It is only small but I found some nice style clothes which I bought. I also got something for you I hope you will like it when I get back.

I also met the counts helper a strange man called Barnaby he had been away. He cooks the meals, and he is a very good cook I will give him that. But he hardly ever speaks, and just stares at you, it is quite unnerving some times.

And the Count never eats he just sits there, and picks at his plate.

Anyway, my darling I will be back shortly the Count is going to buy that property.

I love you always

James Beytagh

Diary of James Beytagh   30th July 2015

I do not know how to put this down in words, but I will try. Last night I wandered the hallways of the castle.

Again, I heard the girls giggling, and went to investigate.

The door handle was smooth under my hand as I turned it, and found that it was open. The room was large with a huge four poster bed, and on the bed were three girls. How can I describe these lovely creatures they were sent from heaven or is that hell?

They took me onto the bed, and began to touch me over all I had three hands on my genitals at one time. Then I felt pain as one sank her teeth into my neck. I was in heaven, and everything felt so good, and then the Count turned up. He was raging, and I swear his eyes were blood red, and his teeth long and sharp.

He cursed at the girls, and they quickly went away.

Then I woke up in my own bed I felt faint all day.

Letter to James Beytagh   28th July 2015

My dearest James

This is so hard for me my darling I am so used to sending e-mails and texts. Snail mail is not for me. Anyway, by the time you get this letter you will probably be home with me. There is not much happening here, my parents went to a party the other night, and dad got drunk as always.

We have had a lot of rain here lately, and my cousins from Southampton visited for a weekend.

Hope to see you soon my darling

Yours

Laura Dillon

Doctor's Diary   15th August 2015

This is a very strange case indeed the man James Beytagh was found asleep on a plane to London. He was hardly conscious, and talked about demons and monsters. I have him in my care now, and have notified his parents. But the man is suffering from delusions, and I had to sedate him.

I will carry on the treatment until I see some improvement.

Doctor Ellis Lyndon asylum

Diary of James Beytagh   21st October 2015

I feel so much better now as I sit on the window sill looking out over the asylum gardens. This has been a trying time for one and all. That cursed castle, and Count haunt my dreams, but I no longer speak of monsters and demons in front of the doctors.

I was so pleased when my Laura visited me yesterday it has been hard for her. She looked well, and said she loved me still, and wanted to marry me.

I am so happy, and I will be going home soon to my fiancé.

E-mail to right sale estate agents   1st November 2015

Dear Greg

I am so much better now, and being home has speeded my recovery. I am just wondering did the Count buy Loughton house.

I hope to be back at work soon if my job is still open to me.

Yours Sincerely

James Beytagh

E-mail to James Beytagh   2nd November 2015

Dear James

Great to hear from you, and I am so glad you are feeling better. Of course, your job is still here for you. And to answer your question yes, the Count did buy Loughton house, and has been there for a couple of months.

Yours sincerely

Greg Carney

Letter to Count Dracula   6th November 2015

Dear Count Dracula

I tired first to find you on social media sites, but nothing then I tried the phone company again a brick wall. But I found you when my employer told me you had in fact bought Loughton house. After what happened to me, I thought you would stay away from England.

I still have nightmares about that stay in your castle, but now I fight my fears. I find myself unable to help myself, and wish to see you again. Would it be possible for me and my fiancée Laura to visit?

Yours Sincerely

James Beytagh

Diary of James Beytagh   17th November 2015

I must be mad that is the only word that I can use for my actions. Why would I want to see the Count again after that terrible visit to his castle?

But I am strong now, and I must face my fears this is my justification.

I know in my heart that the Count is not a man at all, but some vile creature from the depths of hell. But I refuse to fear him, and look forward to seeing him again. Laura will be my strength.

Letter to James Beytagh   21st November 2015

Dear James

I am so glad that you are well my friend, when you became ill at my castle, I was so afraid that you would die.

Barnaby was a great help at that time, and it was he who put you on a plane back to England. I knew I could not get the medical help for you here, and sent you back. As for these fears of yours I know nothing, it was your fever that dreamed up these events.

Thankfully you are okay now, and I would love to see you again, and your fiancé.

Please come this weekend, and I will have Barnaby cook us all a special meal.

Yours sincerely

Count Dracula

Dairy of James Beytagh   26th November 2015

We have come back from the Counts new home an old draftee house. He has not done much to the place, and most rooms are empty. We dined, and again the Count only picked at his food. Was I pleased to see him no I was not?

How dare he say that the fever made me dream all this up I know what I saw in that damned castle. But I acted pleasantly towards him he seemed somehow younger, and more alive.

He took great interest in Laura, and I found this most annoying.

Dairy of Laura Dillon   30th November 2015

How can I put this down in words I am in love, and it is not with James. Oh, I do not wish to hurt my James, but this man is incredible, and took my breath away.

I cannot stop thinking about him since that visit to his home Loughton house. His skin is wrinkled, but his eyes swim with life, and I find him so attractive. I have never gone for the older man before.

When he kissed me good night the kiss was cold, but it lighted up my heart.

Now I must see him again soon.

E-mail to James Beytagh   3rd December 215

Dear James

Please forgive me my darling, but I feel I must have a break for a time. Your illness made me do a lot of thinking. I need some time to myself, and seeing the Count made this stronger.

I will speak to you soon my James

Laura Dillon

Dairy of James Beytagh   3rd December 2015

I received an e-mail from my Laura, and I am afraid. The Count has got her under his wing I just knew it. The way he kept looking at her that night, I must do everything in my power to stop this.

The fiend will surely kill her.

Text to Laura Dillon   4th December 2015

Please Laura my darling do not go to Loughton house alone. The Count is not who he seems.

Love

James Beytagh

Text to James Beytagh

Sorry James, but I am going to Loughton house tonight. Please do not text me again, as I will not answer you.

Laura Dillon

Dairy of James Beytagh   15th December 2015

I finally can sit down and write. How do I start with what happened that night in Loughton house. I went after Laura of course I did she is my one and only sweetheart.

I found her in the arms of the fiend who calls himself the Count. He taunted me at first, and ran his long nails over her throat, and said he wondered how much she would bleed. Barnaby then grabbed me from behind, and held me he was strong.

Then something happened, and the Count seemed to look deep into my very soul. He must have seen the love I had for Laura, and that I was a good man. He let Laura go, and told Barnaby to let me go. The trance Laura was under broke, and she ran into my arms. The Count smiled at me, and told me to leave Loughton house now before he changed his mind. I can tell you I ran all the way home with Laura holding my hand.

The next time I go to Loughton house I will burn the place to the ground.

Kent advertiser   20th January 2016

Deaths births and marriages

Marriage of James Beytagh to Laura Dillon 19th January 2016

Letter to Gerald Grogan   27th December 2015

Dear Mr Grogan

I have recently moved to Scotland, and have found the prefect place for me to stay. I wish to buy castle Robbins in the highlands, and I believe it is your property.

I will offer double what it is worth please reply soon.

Yours sincerely

Count Dracula

Letter to Count Dracula   1st January 2016

Dear Count Dracula

I am so pleased you bought my castle it was just left to decay and ruin. Now I am sure that you will restore it back to its beautiful old self. Please just send me a note to say that you are getting on well.

I will not disturb you again, but only wish that you enjoy Robbins castle.

Yours sincerely

Gerald Grogan

Letter to Gerald Grogan   15th January 2016

Dear Gerald

Thank you for your letter I love the old place, and will look after her.

Please come by one night with your lovely wife Margaret, and have dinner with me. I have my three sisters coming over from Romania to stay with me I am sure you would love to meet them.

Yours sincerely

Count Dracula

The end

C Robert Paul Bennett 2016

25

American vampire vacation

The private jet soared into the night sky now heading over New York.

Inside sitting comfortably were two vampire brothers from the English countryside. The two looked alike, and were around the same height, and build. Both were handsome, and had the look of no worries on their smooth faces. But that could change these two could put on most faces, and some were not very pleasant.

The two brothers had got bored in Allan town, and had left it in the capable hands of their aids back in England. They wanted to spend a little time in America, and see their favourite new pop star in concert.

"You have got those concert tickets brother," Wallace asked.

"Of course, I have I wouldn't miss it for the world," Louis grinned back.

"Good and you got the bus times for the other matter," Wallace asked.

Louis tutted, "Again don't worry brother all our events are in place."

The plane landed, and the two brothers went through the airport, and got a taxi to their hotel.

There was no time to lose the concert was tonight, and the brothers unpacked and had a shower. They sprayed the finest perfumes on their bodies, and dressed in trousers and t-shirts. The t-shirts had the words Cindy Claire in concert, and the concert dates.

"Man, she is the best," Wallace said grinning he hated most new music, but this new kid was good.

"Yes, I'm still surprised that you like her music Wallace," Louis on the other hand enjoyed a wide range of music.

"Don't know why I just like her and her music," Wallace said, and shrugged his shoulders.

"Wow my brother is falling for a human."

"Cut it out Louis," Wallace said with a smile.

"Yes, she is good come on let's get going," Louis said and smiled.

The crowd was getting restless, and Wallace and Louis sat in the expensive seats overlooking the stage.

Wallace looked at his watch she was half an hour late, "Maybe we should go back stage Louis, and see what's happening."

Louis nodded his head, "Come on then."

Her door was locked, and a group of men stood outside calling her name.

"Wallace get everyone into a trance will you," Louis said.

Wallace walked up to the group of men, and they looked at him bad mistake they all went under a trance. Louis kicked in the dressing room door, and went inside, Cindy Claire was on the floor, and she was hardly breathing.

"Fuck it," Louis said and turned to Wallace and said, "You stand guard anyone comes trance them."

Wallace nodded his head, and went to the door way, and stood there. It was a drugs overdose Louis knew straight away, and he picked up the girl in his arms, and sat her down. She had short blonde hair, and blue eyes set in a pale pretty face she wore a light-yellow dress with red boots. He did not have long she was almost dead, and he bit into her white soft neck, and began to drain her of her life's blood.

He cut his wrist, and made her drink his blood, and then lay her on the floor while she changed. She soiled herself, but she opened her eyes, and Louis took her head in his hands, and looked deep into her eyes.

He bonded with her, and told her what she was, and how she would now live. She was a good and strong vampire, and he knew she would do well. She cleaned herself up, and changed her clothes.

"Come Wallace it is done," Louis said walking out of the door.

"Good then let's watch a concert," Wallace walked away, and the group came out of their trance.

The two brothers enjoyed the concert as did hundreds of fans, and it was all in the papers the next day how her concerts had so much energy.

America's most prolific killer was being transferred by security bus to another maximum-security prison. The authorities wanted him far away from his family, and friends. They were getting worried by the amount of people that wanted to visit him. His new prison would be far away. Brady Redman was a large man, and had put on a lot of weight inside prison. He had a bald head, and a mean looking face with a flat nose, and scars across his cheeks.

He had been inside for ten years of a life sentence for killing up to fifty-two women. Strangling them, and raping them.

The figure could be more, but they had no proof that he had murdered other woman. It was rumoured that movie bosses wanted to make a movie of his life this outraged many people. Another reason to move him away, a book on his life had already been scrapped. He sat there, and stared at the guards not moving a muscle.

Wallace and Louis took to the skies as evening began to fall, they could bare a certain amount of sun light. They were old vampires, and had many talents. They saw the security bus, and swooped down like eagles. Wallace landed on the bonnet, and kicked in the window screen.

The driver cried out and lost control, the bus went off the road and into a ditch hitting a large tree. Smoke came out of the engine, and the smell of petrol was heavy in the evening air. Louis dragged the injured security guards away from the burning bus. Wallace grabbed Brady, and then the two brothers took off again as the bus exploded in a ball of fire.

They landed on a tall building, and set the prisoner down on the roof. He shook his head, and looked at the two brothers, "You rescued me thanks my brothers," he said in a cold voice.

"Rescued you I think not," Louis said.

"Why would we rescue a scum bag like you," Wallace added.

"Then what the hell are you going to do with me," Brady said looking from one to the other.

"We are going to gang rape you fucker," Louis hissed in his face.

Brady leaned backwards the man's breath smelt of the grave.

Wallace laughed at the look on Brady's face, "Only joking you silly fucker."

"Then what are you going to do with me," Brady said and for the first time in his unsavoury life he felt fear.

"This," Wallace said and took the man in his arms, and bit into his throat savagely.

Brady struggled for a second then went limp. Wallace cut his wrist, and fed the man his blood. They watched as Brady changed, and soiled his orange boiler suit. There was a strong pole in the centre of the roof, and they tied him tightly to it.

"Hey what the fuck," Brady said he was so hungry for blood.

"The sun will be up in a few hours enjoy my friend," Wallace said, and laughed as he went up into the air.

"Yes, burn you evil little fucker," Louis said, and followed his brother.

They watched from their hotel room the roof was just over the way. The sun came up and they wore their sun glasses, and watched as they heard a scream, and then ashes rose into the air.

The two brothers walked the dark streets a couple of nights later their holiday was almost over.

"What house Wallace you choose this time," Louis said.

Wallace looked at the houses, and reached into them with his mind, and then he smiled, "Number seven I think," he said and marched towards number seven.

They rang the doorbell, and a sweet looking woman answered, and they came into the home, and sat down opposite the young couple. It was easy to get into people's homes you just played with their minds a little.

Shirley was a small woman with ginger hair, and freckles on her cute looking face. Her Husband Tom was tall and thin with a handsome face, and brown hair. The couple were in bad debt, and going to lose their home, there was no way out for them.

Wallace handed over the bag of cash, and unzipped it, and showed it to the young couple.

"Oh my god that's so much money," Shirley said putting her hand over her mouth.

"And it's all yours," Wallace said looking from one to the other.

"Why and who are you," Tom asked.

"Just say we are your guardian angels use the money wisely, and don't waste it," Wallace replied.

"If you abuse the money we will be back," Louis said giving them a hard look.

"Don't worry we will use this money very wisely thank you so much," Shirley said, and she was in tears of joy.

"Yes, thank you," Tom said, but the two men had gone just like that.

Louis and Wallace took their private jet back to London a few nights later. The hostess had such an easy job these two never asked for anything. She was dark haired, and slim with an

Asian looking face, she could not wait to see her boyfriend again.

She missed him, and hoped he would pop the question soon.

Wallace read her mind and smiled he liked her they had used her for flights a few times. All the cabin crew and pilots were human, and worked for the brothers.

They landed at London, and quickly went through customs, and out into the chilly night. They got a taxi back to the countryside town of Allan.

"Well, it was a lovely break Wallace," Louis said sighing he was looking forward to a long sleep in his coffin.

"Yes, I must say I enjoyed that very much," Wallace replied.

Once they got back the two vampires looked over the town of Allan all was quiet. Then they went down into the basement, and got into their coffins the helpers were already asleep.

"Good night brother," Wallace said closing his coffin lid.

"Good night, Wallace," and Louis followed suit.

The end

C Robert Paul Bennett 2016

26

The vampire help line

There is a radio station that can be picked up by a few in the know, it is on a channel that not many people can find or are bothered to find.

Caller= "I can't go on any longer this life is boring me so much."

VHL= "Please sir calm down, and tell me slowly what your problem is."

Caller= "I have lived a long time, and now after so many decades I grow tired. There is no sense to a life as a vampire, you never get old and people die around you."

VHL= "Sorry sir but that's the way it has always been for our kind."

The voice of the radio DJ was smooth and sexy a woman's voice.

Caller= "Yes maybe be that is true, but can you help me at all please I am going crazy."

VHL= "Okay sir what we vampires do when we are bored is we go underground."

Caller= "I have heard about this tell me more."

VHL= "You must find a safe place a crypt or a tomb of some kind, and then go to sleep."

Caller= "How will I wake up again, and wont I be weak."

VHL= "Of course you will be weak get a fellow vampire who you can trust, and they will wake you, and feed you blood."

Caller= "Well I must say that sounds good thank you so much."

VHL= "You are so welcome sir."

2

Caller= "I am so sick of animal blood I want to go out and hunt humans."

VHL= "Yes sir we all want to do that, but its best we don't draw attention to ourselves."

Caller= "There must be a way I can't stand this animal blood anymore."

VHL= "There is a way, but you only do this for a short while then go back on animal blood okay."

Caller= "Okay tell me."

VHL= "You can choose a human to feed on night after night, but only take a small amount of their blood. Then leave them be and go back to animal blood for a few months, then chose another human for a feed."

Caller= "Thank you so much I will give that a try."

VHL= "You are most welcome."

3

Caller= "I am a woman vampire, and get most of my clients by dressing up as a hooker, and luring them in. I am sick of being a vampire hooker, and sick of overweight perverts."

VHL= "I can see why you are upset I wouldn't like to dress up as a hooker to get blood."

Caller= "Yes, it is degrading for a vampire, and like you said in your last call I only drain them a bit."

VHL= "That's great I'm glad to hear that."

Caller= "So can you help me."

VHL= "Yes of course I can its simple use a bit of money, and buy a business be a business woman in a suit."

Caller= "Why that is a splendid idea I will try that thank you."

VHL= "You are most welcome, and good luck on the new venture."

4

Caller= "I know we don't like to kill humans because it could draw attention to us, but I have a real problem."

VHL= "Please go on sir."

Caller= "I have a real vampire hunter, and he is getting closer."

VHL= "Yes this could be a problem have you seen him, and has he seen you."

Caller= "Yes he carries stakes and garlic around in a bag can you believe that shit."

The caller laughs.

Caller= "Yes he has seen me feeding on a cow."

VHL= "Okay he sounds tame enough go ahead and kill him, but make sure you get rid of the body."

Caller= "Thank you so much this man is becoming a pain."

VHL= "I agree we can do without humans like him."

Caller= "Well thank you for the advice, and the go ahead."

VHL= "You are welcome, sir."

5

Caller= "Hello radio vampire."

The caller starts laughing.

VHL= "How can I help you sir."

Caller= "This is such a load of shit I found your radio station, and I am going to reveal you for what you really are."

VHL= "Really sir, and what am I."

Caller= "A woman who is just making money on simple people who believe they are vampires it's well sick."

VHL= "I do not make any money, and sir are you a vampire."

Caller= "No of course I'm not there is no such thing, and you know that."

VHL= "I don't know anything of the kind sir."

Caller= "Oh please stop the act I am outside, and I am going to come inside, and put you off the air once and for all."

VHL= "By all means please do sir."

On the radio you can hear a door opening, and a man's voice cursing. Then there is pause, and then a man can be heard screaming.

VHL= "Next caller please."

The end

C Robert Paul Bennett 2016

27

Vampire town

The small town sat in the mountains a long winding road led up to the town, but they did not have that many visitors. In the summer you would get a few tourists the town was so picturesque. It had brick houses lined up along tree lined streets. It was always kept clean, and you never saw stray animals.

The town's population was vampires, and human slaves with pets of course. During the day it was the human slave's job to look after the pets, and keep the town clean. Night town as was its name only came alive at night time.

But it was all above board, and they paid their taxes, and all worked in night town. It was one big family, and they never drew attention to themselves.

Dave and Joanne smiled as they looked on at little Jack, he was a boy full of mischief. Dave was tall and thin with short brown hair, and a dimple in his chin. His wife Joanne had long dark hair, and a button nose on her pretty face. Their son Jack had been dying in a children's ward in the big city when they had saved him as their own.

Now they would be a family forever in night town.

Jack started to play with the cat Busby, and the proud parents smiled as he stroked the cat. Then the boy picked up the cat and showed his long fangs, "No," shouted Dave and ran for the cat.

He picked up the cat before the boy could sink his teeth into it.

"Bad Jack what have we told you, no biting family members," Dave scolded the little boy.

He went all tearful and said, "Sorry dad."

Joanne took the little boy in her arms, "Now love, Busby is a member of our family, and we don't feed on family members do we."

"No mum I'm sorry," the little boy gave a half-hearted smile.

"Now go and say sorry to Busby," Dave said smiling at his son.

The little boy went over and picked up the black and white moggy, and hugged him and kissed him, "Sorry Busby."

Of course, some humans did come to night town asking questions. Why did the town only come to life at night etc?

But most of the residents had a disease they could not face sun light it was rare, but it brought them all together. The humans would go away and check this up, and find it to be true, and the people paid their taxes.

That is when the tourist started to come in small numbers night town intrigued them. A town full of people who could not go in the sun light. A news paper article had started all that, but the towns folk did not mind it brought in money. The infamous night town became vampire town to many people.

Every member of night town had a job inside the town, no one worked outside. There was a book store run by one family a DVD store, coffee shop, and burger bar. A gift shop, and a barber, and library. A steak house restaurant, and even a bowling alley, and hotel of course. A mini market for vegetables, and meat and fish etc.

They allowed the tourist to stay, but no one ever became a resident from outside. Each opened at night, and stayed open till late morning then the town would return to a ghost town.

But there was a special super market that was only for residents. The market had fresh animal's blood in cartons, and frozen animal's blood. Frozen blood lollipops, and hard-boiled blood drop sweets. There was vintage blood in bottles which cost a bit more of course.

There was also cheap bottled blood, and if you were rich a selection of fine bottled human blood. If there was a party or celebration the town's folk would buy these, but that was rare.

One day a man came to town he was tall and thin with spots on his face. He had lank brown hair and oily skin, and shifty eyes. He knocked on a door at random, and it was answered by a small bald man who looked a bit like uncle fester from the Munster's.

"Hello sir can I help you," the small bald man asked.

The man pushed his way in, and then the bald man was on his back. They wrestled, and the man fell to the floor. He went backwards, and the bald man hit his head hard.

The thin man got to his feet, and looked down at the unconscious man and smiled.

"These bastards are vampires," he spat out.

He did not believe the story for one minute about them being diseased, and knew they were vampires, and he was going to prove it. He was a young man lacking in intelligence. He found the basement door and opened it, and saw the stairs going down into the dark. He took out a flash light. He moved down the stairs, and came to a long corridor that leads to a door. He walked down there were no windows down here.

He opened the door and walked inside, and saw the coffins lined up against one wall.

"Yes, I knew it," he said in triumph.

The coffin lids opened and Dave and Joanne looked at the young man and smiled, "Diner time," Dave said.

The man screamed as the vampire family took hold of him, no one could hear him down here. Dave fed on the boy's neck and Joanne took a wrist, the kid Jack bit into the young man's calf. They all fed well that day, and would not need to go to the special super market.

Well maybe they would pick up some blood sweets for Jack. The bald man upstairs rubbed the back of his head, and smiled. He heard the man's screams from the top of the stairs. He closed the basement door, and took out the Hoover time for some house work.

The end

C Robert Paul Bennett 2016

28

Vampire united

When a team called vampire united entered the annual five a side football tournament no one raised an eye lid. Why would they when you had teams called the sea serpents, and the devils eleven etc.

The tournament was held in the evenings so people could get home from work. The tournament went on for a week. The teams had to pay to enter, and won a nice trophy, and medals for winning.

The tall man stood in front of his team and smiled they were going to win this no matter what. The other vampires looked on at him they were all dressed in their kits. Red tops, and white shorts with the words vampire united on the backs. The goalkeeper was chubby there were two lanky ones, and a small dwarfish one. There were two substitutes these were of medium height.

"Right lads we will cheat to get to the final okay," the captain said.

"We can use our powers then," a chubby vampire asked.

"Yes, but only mind control don't let the crowd see anything weird okay," the captain answered.

They all nodded, "But," the captain said raising his hand.

"When we get to the final, we must win it fairly no powers at all agreed," he said, and looked round the dressing room.

"Agreed," they all said as one.

It was easy for the team at first, they raced away with a 36-0 win in the first round, and a 41-0 in the second round.

But then they eased off a bit, and won 21-0 in the third round and 13-0 in the quarter finals.

The semi finals they just took it easy, and played around with the team for a while, they won 15-0.

There were a few remarks from watching fans like 'our team are like zombies' or 'they look like they're not even trying.'

So, it came to the final.

The final match up was against the pond dwellers, and no powers at all were to be used. The game was hard fought, and at one time it was level at 2-2. At the half time whistle it was 5-4 to vampire united.

But the team the pond dwellers played their hearts out, but the vampire team never ran out of energy, and never got tired.

In the end the pond dwellers just ran out of steam, and the vampires won 12-7 in a close final. At the whistle the vampires hugged their human opponents, and wished them well for next year. The captain lifted the trophy, and the players got their medals.

That was the last time anyone ever saw vampire united they never showed up again for the tournament again.

And the next year the pond dwellers won the final over the sea serpents 10-9.

The end

C Robert Paul Bennett 2016

29

Varney the vampire

The fat stage manager sat on a chair, and put his head in his hands.

It was 19th century Paris, and the people needed shows to take their minds off war, and hard ships. He was running out of ideas, and needed something to bring back the crowds. He was a big fat man who enjoyed his food and drink far too much. He had a bald head, and a moustache, and wrinkles in his face.

"What I'm I to do," he whispered, and a wind whipped across his body, and he looked up.

The man was tall and thin like a rake with long dark hair, and black eyes in a pale white face. He wore clothes of black and a cloak around his shoulders. He handed the fat man a manuscript, and the fat man looked at it in his hands.

"What's this, and who are you my friend," the stage manager asked.

"Who I am is not important, but read and see if you like," the man answered in a deep voice.

"Okay my friend I will read your manuscript, but I fear nothing can bring back the crowds," the fat man said with a sigh.

"We shall see," said the man, and then he was gone.

The stage manager looked at the title on the manuscript Varney the vampire.

The fat stage manager was excited he had read the manuscript twice, and ideas were forming in his head. The play would be a huge success he just knew it would. The story ended, but there was no author. A show about a vampire how new was that the people would love it, and the crowds would come again.

The tall thin man in the clock watched the show with the people, and the crowds did come back. At first it was slow, but once word got around people could not wait to see the unusual play.

The dark-haired man smiled as he watched the play, he liked what the stage manager had done with his story. A man approached him, "I am a struggling author the stage manager pointed you out to me."

"Yes, sir and how may I help you," replied the cloaked man in black.

"Can I write a book using your story I will do a good job of it I swear."

The man in black smiled, "Of course you can sir."

And that is how Varney the vampire came to be, and with an author at last.

The show ran for many years, and the book was at first in the form of a kind of penny dreadful. The book ended up being a very long book, and now is very rare indeed. There are still posters around for Varney the vampire, and you may find these on the internet.

The end

C Robert Paul Bennett 2016

30

Fang's

It was almost sun rise, and the creature had been caught out, where could it hide. Then it saw the sewer man hole cover, and quickly lifted the cover, and almost fell into the hole. The creature closed the man hole cover, and sighed that was close a few more seconds, and it would have been ashes. The creature went down into the sewer, and searched around until it found a place in a small corridor. This would have to be its home for tonight anyway, and then see what happens.

Arnold had worked in the sewers for twenty plus years, and was looking forward to retirement. He and his wife could travel the world just like they promised themselves. Arnold was sixty-two with grey hair and a well trimmed beard he was a podgy man, and had two chins on his fat face. He enjoyed a pint down the local pub with his mates, and had a weakness for Chinese take away food. Every Saturday night it was Chinese take away, and a movie, and a few beers with his wife.

He sighed better check this part of the sewer it was old, and had to be checked regularly. He shone his light and saw a small corridor off to the left this was old, and he had not really been down this part much. Normally he would be with Pete his partner, but he was off sick today.

He moved into the dark space, and paused he heard a noise in front of him, and shone his light. He gasped as the light shone on a mouth full of teeth with two long fangs, He screamed as the creature took him.

Little Johnny and Logan laughed as they came to the entrance of a sewer pipe it ran into a small stream. Johnny was ten and had short brown hair, and a cute face he wore shorts, and a sweat shirt. Logan was also ten, but much larger than Johnny with dark hair, he too wore shorts and a t-shirt with U2 on the front.

"Come on let's go inside," Johnny said, and lay down on his front on his skate board.

"Wicked we can wheel ourselves in," Logan replied and followed suit. The two boys pushed themselves along on their skate boards with Johnny up front.

"Hey I don't like this I'm getting wet," Logan said the water splashing up at him.

"Be quiet I heard something," Johnny said from the front.

Logan looked he could just make out Johnny's body, and then Johnny screamed! It was a fearsome sound, and sent shivers through Logan's young body. Logan cried out and left his skate board, and ran for the sunlight as if all the devils from hell were after him.

This was a small town, and the police force consisted of Curt and two constables who were busy rescuing a cat from a tree. So, Curt took this job, and he looked into the dark sewer. He was a man of medium height and build with short dark hair, and green eyes set in a handsome face. He had been on the town's police force since he left school fifteen years ago, and enjoyed his work.

It was not to taxing, and the town never had any murders only stray dogs biting or cats in trees. The sewer ran into a small stream, and he entered the sewer pipe, and went into it in a crouch. He shone his torch, and soon found a skate board. He picked it up and examined it yes this was Logan's, he said it had U2 rule on it the boys loved the band U2.

Then he saw Johnny's skate board, but it had been snapped into two pieces. He picked up the pieces something strong done this. He moved back into the sunlight, and away from the sewer, and put the skate boards in his car.

Thomas was a large man with a huge beer belly sticking out in front of him. He had a red jolly face and a smile. He shook Curt's hand.

"Hi Thomas I got a small boy missing last seen in this sewer," Curt said to the big smiling man.

Thomas oversaw this part of the sewer, and knew it well, "That's strange Curt because we have a missing sewer worker also," Thomas said rubbing his fat chin.

"I need to go in deep," Curt said.

Thomas handed him a pair of rubber boots and gloves, and a strong flash light. "Put these on, and we will be on our way."

The two men splashed through the sewer water, and went deeper into the tunnels. It was dark and smelly, and occasionally Curt would gag.

"Been working these tunnels all my life seen some pretty weird shit as well," Thomas said in a jolly voice.

"Really," Curt was a little unnerved as it was down here without stories.

"Seen a rat as big as a great Dane dog I'm telling you," Thomas said and laughed, "I think it was down these tunnels as well."

"Please Thomas enough," Curt said moving slowly through the cold water.

"Mind you I have heard rumours of rats even bigger than that, and killer leeches.

We had an outbreak of killer leeches do you remember that Curt," Thomas asked.

"Can't say I do Thomas," Curt said with a sigh.

"Bad times like vampires they were sucking the blood out of people," Thomas laughed again.

Curt saw a black thin thing in the water and gasped, "What's that," he said in fear thinking of killer leeches.

Thomas laughed and picked it up, "It's only a piece of rubber."

They moved on farther, and then Curt stopped and picked up a hard hat, and showed it to Thomas.

Thomas looked at the serial number, "This is Arnolds the missing sewer worker."

Then Thomas pointed to a small tunnel leading off to the left, "We should look in there."

Thomas took the lead, and went into the small space, Curt waited in the larger tunnel. Thomas shone his light, and gasped as he saw a large mouth full of teeth, and two long fangs.

"What the fuck," he cursed, and then the thing took him.

Curt heard water splashing, and something drop and stepped into the small space, and shone his light round. The space was like a small room built into the sewer, and there was another tunnel leading away. He saw Thomas flash light in the water, and picked it up. The light went out, and he dropped it again there was no sign of Thomas.

He thought about giant rats, and shivered what if one came out of the tunnel now, and chased him. He would have no chance he was sitting duck here. He turned and walked back the way he had come, and then kicked something in the water. He stopped, and shone his flash light down, and saw Thomas staring up at him.

Something had ripped his head off and Curt bent over, and was violently sick. Thoughts of giant rats fresh in his mind he began to ran in fear.

Curt ran, and started to cry out he could feel the tunnel walls closing in on him. He sank to his knees in the dirty water panting, and trying to get his breath back. He heard a noise in front of him, and shone his flash light, there was a man standing in front of him. He was pale and wore black clothes he had dark hair which was long, and small dark eyes. His hands hang at his sides, and he had sharp long nails.

Then the man opened his mouth, he had a mouth full of teeth, and two long wicked looking fangs. Curt got to his feet and faced the man, "Please spare me," he begged.

The man in black swiped his hand across Curt's throat, and Curt felt blood pumping out of the wound. His blood sprayed across the sewer wall. The man in black took him in his arms, and put his face into his throat.

The end

C Robert Paul Bennett 2016

31

The healing vampire

The rain poured down onto the English countryside, the rain had not stopped for weeks, and everything was soaked. This was eighteenth century England, and times were hard, and the people weather beaten and strong of spirit.

Joey was sixteen, and small for his age he had short messy blonde hair, and a cute angel like face. He wore trousers made by his mother from rough cloth and tied with string his shirt was the same. His old boots were full of holes, and as he walked in the rain, he felt sorry for himself. He was tired, and hungry, and now wet.

He was getting soaked to his skin, and saw a large oak tree and hurried over to it, the tree would offer him shelter from the down pouring rain. He saw that the trunk of the oak tree had a hollow in its side good for playing go hide and seek he thought. He leaned against the trunk of the old tree, and let out a deep sigh. The rain could not get at him now only drips. Then his arm was gripped by a strong hand, and he gasped and looked down. The hand was red raw, and burnt like the sides of meat his father would cook over the open fire.

"Don't be scared boy I need your help," a deep sounding voice said from the hollow of the tree.

The boy was not afraid, and the hand let him go, "Who are you sir," he asked in his sweet voice.

"I am a man who has done no wrong, but been punished we are all god's creatures are we not boy."

"Yes, sir we are, and for that reason I will help you," the truth was Joeys life was so boring helping on his parent's farm all day.

This on the other hand sounded exciting, and maybe dangerous.

"Good boy what's your name," asked the voice from the tree hollow.

"I am Joey, and who are you sir."

"I am Vladimir, and I have travelled far."

"Where are you from sir your English is good."

"That does not matter my little friend, but you help me and I will give you and your family riches."

The boy smiled his family was so poor this would change all that.

"Now come here Joey, and do not be afraid I will harm you not."

Joey came closer to the hollow, and a man stepped out of it he smelt of burnt meat. He wore tatty dark clothes that were badly burnt. The flesh on his face was red raw, and dark in patches his lips were burnt off, and his teeth showed. Joey was scared at first but forced himself to stand there, and not run away. The man leaned over, and whispered into his ear.

Joey walked through the forest the next day, and the rain was only light today, but the clouds looked dark and ominous. He was holding a pig he had stolen from his father's pig pen he would just say the pig escaped. The fencing round the pen was old and worn wood.

He came to the old oak tree, and walked up to the hollow, "Sir I have a pig for you."

A hand came out of the hollow, and Joey handed over the rope. The pig was pulled to the hollow, and then pulled inside. Joey stood there and heard the pig squeal, and then sucking noises. The pig's drained carcass was thrown out of the hollow, and the voice told him, "Now get rid of the body for me and bring me more animals."

Joey did as he was told, and buried the pig in loose soil close by.

The boy came back to the hollow of the tree and the voice said, "If you are to be my friend then I must show you something, and you will understand."

"Okay sir," Joey said and moved closer.

A burnt hand shot out and held his hand, and Joey saw a vision in his young mind.

The dark man was running through the forest in the rain the villagers had found him at last. He had been hiding out in a crypt in the graveyard for months now. He had been feeding on the villager's animals to survive, but he had left them alone. But they were poor people, and the loss of animals hit them hard. They chased the dark clothed man, and cursed at him and called him what he was 'vampire,' they held sticks and forks and shovels.

It was almost day light, and the figure in dark clothes knew he had to find a hide out very soon. But it was too late, and the villagers were right behind him as he came out of the trees, and onto a cliff on top of the hill. He stood at the cliff, and looked down it was very far down.

The villagers stopped, and surrounded him as the sun came out, and burnt his body he screamed, and they cheered.

He opened his arms wide and fell of the cliff, and screamed all the way down. Lucky for him he fell into a hole in the ground that led to an underground cave. He rested for many days letting his body recover, but it was slow, and he needed blood to heal faster. He walked through the forest and found the hollowed out oak tree, and rested inside. He would sleep for a long time, and maybe when he woke his body would be hungry but healed.

"Then you came along Joey," the man said.

"Wow you are a vampire sir."

"Yes, but as you saw I harmed no one in that village I am one of god's creatures as well, and need blood to survive."

"I will make you strong again sir I am a good hunter I will bring you blood."

"You're a good boy Joey."

Over the next few days Joey caught rabbits and squirrels, and gave them to the man in the hollow. He ate well, and they chatted about things that were not important. Joey held the three rabbits, and came to the hollow tree and stopped, the man was outside leaning against the trunk.

"Sir you must be careful you will burn," Joey said, and handed over the rabbits.

"Do not worry my friend the clouds offer good cover from the sun light."

The man was getting better his skin was started to look like skin again, and his lips were growing back.

"Vladimir you are growing strong again I can see it," Joey said with a smile on his cute little face.

"Yes, but I need something more Joey."

"Tell me sir, and I will get for you."

"I need a man."

Joey thought about this, and he had an idea the vampire would need a man soon to recover fully, and he knew just the person.

"I can do that Vladimir."

"Make sure he is a bad man of mind and spirit I leave good people alone."

"Oh yes sir this man is very bad."

The man Joey was after sat in the inn drinking himself into a trance like state. The man was fat and had a red face that looked like it would burst at any minute. Joey sat opposite the man, and smiled at him.

"What do you want boy," the man slurred at him the smell of stale beer was strong.

"I need money sir," Joey said in his sweetest voice.

If ever you needed money, and were young this man would give you a little, but he would rape you first he was a pervert of the highest order preying on the young poor boys.

"Good then come back to my place," the man slurred.

"No sir I know a better place where no one will see us."

He took the drunken man into the forest, and the man kept on cursing, "Where the devil are you taking me."

"Not far now sir," Joey would say.

They came to the hollow oak tree, "This is my hide out sir step in there's room for both of us."

The drunk looked at the large hollow and grumbled, and climbed inside.

He screamed once, and then was silent Joey heard the sucking noises, and they went on for longer this time. The drained body came out, and then out stepped Vladimir. He looked so much better and his skin had a health look, but still he had patches of burnt skin, and his hands were still burnt.

"You have done well Joey I am almost well again."

"Yes, sir you do look better."

"I will dispose of the body this time you my friend go home."

Joey took a short cut to the old oak tree the next day, and ran through the forest of trees and bushes. The sun was out for once, and it made him feel in high spirits. He almost tripped over something, and stopped and looked down. There were two men hiding under some leaves and under growth. Joey got a better look, and gasped they were dead and pale, and drained of blood, Vladimir had done this. The two men were soldiers from the nearby town.

He raced to the old oak tree, and went up to the hollow, "Ah my friend I'm glad you came."

"Vladimir did you kill those two men."

"Ah Joey, you found them I'm sorry about that but yes, and now I am ready to leave this place."

"You are leaving."

"Yes, but first I will reward you tonight."

Vladimir showed Joey his face just in the light enough the man was handsome and all healed up, and his hands were healed.

The soldiers sneered down at Joey's dad from their horses, "Pay your taxes now or we burn down your farm."

His father was a tall thin man with a balding head, and a swallow looking cheek bones. The man who spoke looked evil with his dark hair, and scars across his ugly face.

"In the name of the king we demand your taxes now peasant," the evil man spat at his father. Joey was in the door way with his mother looking on.

"I have no money to give you sir," his father pleaded with the three men.

"Then prepare to die," the evil man said, and drew his sword.

Then he was gone one minute he was on his horse with sword in hand, and the next he was missing. The two other soldiers looked at each other then at Joey's father. Then another man was gone, and then the last man.

The three horses stood there without their riders, and a man in dark clothes appeared, and smiled at Joey. It was Vladimir, and he looked so handsome in his new clothes.

"The soldiers are dead, and their property is now yours my friend," Vladimir said to Joey's father.

"I don't know what to say sir," his father would not look a gift horse in the face.

Vladimir handed Joeys father saddles of money from the horses there was enough to last a life time for the family.

"I will take the horses they are marked as soldier horses, and you take the money, and move on somewhere better."

"Thank you, sir," Joey's father said almost in tears of joy.

"Thank you, kindly sir," Joey's mother ran to the darkly clothed man, and kissed him on his cold cheek.

Joey hugged the man and said, "I will always remember you Vladimir."

"I too my little friend," Vladimir put his hand through the boy's hair, and smiled down at him.

He took the horses and waved good bye to the family. He let two of the horses go after burying the three soldiers, and kept one for himself.

He rode off into the night, and headed he knew not where.

The end

C Robert Paul Bennett 2016

Made in the USA
Columbia, SC
24 February 2024

32234843R00115